RANCHER NEXT DOOR

PART-TIME COWBOYS, BOOK 4

MARIE JOHNSTON

LE PUBLISHING

Two years ago, Lucas's high-school sweetheart divorced him for her boss, leaving him with nothing but a string of words like *unreliable, disappointing,* and *failure.* He hasn't looked at another woman since—a failing farm and an ailing dad are all he has time for. But when an old friend moves back next door, he can't help but notice she's a woman. And single. And ignoring him.

Seven years ago, Trina's boyfriend left her for greener pastures, leaving her nothing but a son and no child support to help raise him. So when she's late for the interview of a lifetime and the childhood friend who abandoned her offers to cover, she can't afford to say no. The proposal is clear: pretend to date him and she'll get the job she needs with his aunt.

They both know the deal. It should be no problem. But the more Lucas learns about Trina's plans and ambitions, the more he knows his ex-wife was right—he has nothing to offer. Yet the bigger the glimpse Trina gets into Lucas's lonely life, the more she wants to be a part of it, even at the risk of her own damaged heart. These old friends have so much more to risk the second time around, but the temptation next door has never looked so good.

CHAPTER 1

*I*f her neighbor didn't turn down his music, Trina was going to march over there and—

What? Ogle how well his jeans molded to his ass? Lick her lips as her gaze strayed to his wide shoulders? Admire how the lanky kid she'd grown up with had bulked out?

Lucas Peterson wasn't male-model material by any means. Bordering on stocky, he rocked the dad bod without having any kids. But even a little padding couldn't hide his muscles, or the twinkle in his eye when he ordered a beer while she was on shift.

Trina punched her pillow and flipped over. Maybe it was because she had a kid that a dad bod had suddenly captured her attention. She'd known Lucas her whole life. They'd been close once. Before—

Heavy bass pounded through the air into her open window.

Moving in with Mom and Sarah might not have been the best idea. Her crappy apartment at least had AC. June shouldn't be this fucking hot anyway.

But it wouldn't be so bad if Lucas would shut his music

off. Then she could sleep. Her early-morning appointment was too critical to mess up. She *needed* to sleep.

With a huff, she rolled up and staggered out of bed. It was after midnight, and while these were normal hours for her bartender job, she had to get used to waking up even earlier than she usually did to get Brayden to school.

Irritation whispered through her, and she used all the recent run-ins with Lucas to fuel it. The way he teased her about her close-cropped hair. The way he threw out a borderline insult every time she walked by. The way he had to call out after her for another beer in the bar when she ignored him. What were they, ten? It's like they were trying to outdo each other using words that'd get her relegated to manure duty if Mom ever overheard.

The challenge in his voice whenever he commented on her service? It was the same tone he'd used when they'd raced to see who could catch the most grasshoppers.

"Fucking Lucas," she growled as she tossed on a hoodie over her nightshirt. The shorts would be fine. A row of scraggly trees separated his property from hers but didn't provide much of a sound buffer. She'd probably find him in the detached garage closest to the trees.

She left her room and stopped in the little office-turned-bedroom to check on Brayden. He was sprawled across the bed, having shed the covers sometime during the night. Rusty Rivets pajamas covered his seven-year-old body. Between those and Paw Patrol, he didn't vary a whole lot in his style.

Confident he was fast asleep, she stormed out of the house, pausing only long enough to slip her Vans on.

As she charged across the drive, the frogs living in the runoff-filled ditches paused at the racket she made stomping through the gravel. The crickets didn't let up though. If she couldn't strike fear in the heart of a tiny bug, then how was she going to face Lucas?

No, she stared down men for a living. Wrestled keys away after they'd had too many and still insisted they were just fine driving home. Stepped into the middle of altercations, usually over something dumb like a guy talking to someone's girl. And picked grown men up off the floor when they'd passed out in the bathroom.

She could do this.

Between her yard light and Lucas's, she circled around the row of short trees in the dark without twisting an ankle. Sarah had talked about planting fresh saplings later this year. In ten years, they might have a natural privacy fence.

The lights in the garage gave it a life of its own, flickering along with the Jason Aldean song blaring into the night. Every so often, metal clanged against the floor. What the hell was the guy working on at midnight?

She veered around to the front and planted her hands on her hips. The garage door was wide open. Between the tunes and his concentration, he hadn't heard her approach. His back was to her as he bent over the engine of an old Chevy pickup. It was the one that his dad had gotten him. He used to drive it as a teenager until, after graduation, he'd bought a ridiculously expensive new truck to please his stupid girlfriend who'd turned into his wife.

Trina had felt sorry for him when he'd gotten divorced, but she'd also really wanted to slap him. The idiot should've known better than to think Shaylee would do anything less than she'd done—sleep with her boss. The girl had been superficial out of the womb, probably complaining about the low thread count of the blanket that received her.

"Lucas," she barked.

His shoulders tightened like she'd startled him, but he didn't whip around. Instead, he grabbed the beer that was sitting on the fender and took a slow, lazy pull before turning to face her.

His blue T-shirt was old and faded. Oil and grease smears decorated both the shirt and his jeans. He lowered the beer bottle from his lips and shot her a playful, crooked grin.

"Well, well, well. If Trina Hart isn't gracing my property once again. To what do I owe the honor?"

The way her traitorous stomach flipped was shameful. It had to be the lack of sleep. Not the way his shirt clung to his frame. He didn't have a definitive beer gut, more like beer padding. It wasn't enough to hide his body. Certainly not enough to conceal the bulge of his biceps.

Meanwhile, she'd lost the extra lift pregnancy had given her boobs, but her childbearing hips were still in place.

She used that unfairness to fuel her anger. "Your music's too loud."

He took another languid swig. His gaze traveled down to her gray Vans and back up her bare legs to her face. He didn't linger on her chest or push the line of lewdness. Just stark appreciation for the parts he could see.

Damn him. She shouldn't revel in his reaction.

"I would think you're used to it, Tree-bee." His nickname for her slammed up her defenses. They'd been best friends. Buddies. Tied at the hip. When they weren't doing chores, they'd been running together across their bordering lands. Then he'd hit high school. Navigated puberty. And instead of growing closer and maybe showing more than brotherly interest, he'd ditched her. Hung out with the guys, started dating, and then followed Shaylee like a needy puppy. All while pretending she'd never existed.

Ass.

"Turn it down." She folded her arms over her bulky sweater. Maybe she should've put on a bra.

"Why? Your moms are gone for the week."

Some of her anger faded. When he referred to her moms, there was never a hint of taunting in his voice, or condescension, or disapproval. He'd known her dad back when they were actually friends, and he'd also been her sounding board after Dad had abandoned her.

"Mom and Sarah might be gone but— Wait, how do you know?"

"Sarah asked me to take care of the cattle."

"I can do it. I'm living here now."

His smile died. "What happened?"

"None of your business." That made it sound more mysterious than the truth: she needed to save money to go to nursing school. *If* she got into nursing school. It'd help to have more experience than bartending, and her appointment tomorrow was critical. "Turn down the music."

He smirked, the same one that he gave her in the bar when he made a caustic remark to get under her skin. Him just *being* in the bar got under her skin.

"No." Now he was almost smiling.

This was a game to him. Her future was riding on the line. The opportunities she could afford for her son were hanging in the balance. Maybe she'd built tomorrow up to be more than it was, but it didn't feel like it. Her options where limited.

"Lucas—" She sighed. "I'm trying to get some rest. I have to work tomorrow."

"Then go home and get to bed." There was that grin. Slightly lopsided, framed by shadowy stubble. "Do you need me to tuck you in?"

Her body tingled and the word "yes" hovered on her lips like she'd lost her damn mind. "Brayden needs to get up early. You want to wake him up in the middle of the night—"

Her words died as Lucas crossed to the workbench on his left and flicked the radio off. Lifting his maroon ball cap and running a hand over his russet-brown hair, he lifted a brow, challenging her.

"Thanks," she gritted out. It was sweet that he did as she asked once she mentioned Brayden. But he'd still ignored *her*.

"My offer to tuck you in is still good."

Surprise surged again. Lucas had never been so bold in the bar. Nor had he ever—*ever*—shown any interest beyond riling her up. "Good night, Lucas." She pivoted to march away, then turned back. "Why the hell are you working this late at night anyway?"

The teasing glint was still in his eyes, but this time it seemed forced. "Because I can. I'm a bachelor."

Sympathy tugged at her heartstrings. She hadn't liked Shaylee, but the stages of grief she'd witnessed Lucas go through at the bar had been awful. She thought he'd settled on acceptance, but maybe she'd been wrong.

"Living the dream?" she asked lightly.

His gaze swept the garage and his jaw tightened. The house had an attached garage, but this single-stall structure was original to the property and a lot older. The mustiness of old wood was interspersed with grease smells. The dirt-packed floor looked better off than the peeling panel walls. "Living someone's dream. Look, if I woke Brayden, I'm sorry."

A freight train passing ten feet from the house couldn't wake Brayden. Not much did. The kid had learned to sleep anywhere and through anything when they'd lived in town. "As long as there's no thunder, he should be fine."

The corner of Lucas's mouth hitched up. "The kid's afraid of storms?"

She nodded. The conversation had entered dangerous territory. She should stay angry with him. Ignore him. But she couldn't be friends with him again. Getting ditched once or three or ten times had convinced her of that. "I have an early meeting. Good night, Lucas."

As she walked away, he called, "Why'd you move back?"

She pretended she didn't hear him and kept walking.

~

STARING AT THE POPCORN CEILING, Lucas sprawled across his bed. How many times had he replayed the encounter with Trina last night? Or was it this morning?

Four hours of sleep later, he couldn't drift off again.

She'd looked…approachable. At Barley 'n' Hops, she was constantly on the move. Darting here, stopping to take orders there. Clearing tables, getting change—she had so many options that didn't include talking to him, and she used them.

That sweater. Had she thought it'd hide the fact that she wasn't wearing a bra? Did she think that just because she didn't have more tits than a guy could palm that he couldn't tell whether they were swinging free and accessible? Because she'd be wrong.

So. Wrong.

He knew. Like he knew when her right knee ached from the hitch in her step as she maneuvered tables in the bar. A four-wheeler incident when they were six had left her with a busted kneecap that hadn't been discovered broken until six weeks and a lot of pain later. But then, her dad hadn't been big on doctors—and he'd been the one driving the ATV.

He liked Sarah so much better than Nathan Hart. Sarah was better for Trina and her mom, Davina, than Nathan cared to be. And Sarah could ranch circles around anyone but his friends the Walkers. Together with Davina, they made their ranch profitable.

Sarah helped him on the farm too, or he'd be lobbing

money out the window. Farming was hard by himself. He glanced at the clock. If he went to town now, he could meet Dad for breakfast. It didn't take long to dress and stagger into the kitchen. If he wanted to eat, he had to do it now. Breakfast with Dad was…

He downed two pieces of dry toast and a glass of orange juice. On his way to town, he drove slow past the Hart ranch. Trina's car must be in the garage.

She was living next door again. Huh.

Last night, she'd been wearing shorts. She wasn't tall, but her legs were long, and definitely not the spindly twigs they'd been as a kid. Tree-bee. She was always buzzing around. Each time he saw her in the bar, he thought of that nickname. Moving here and there, taking care of everyone and getting little thanks for it.

He pulled into the parking lot where Dad lived. It wasn't even eight a.m. yet.

Yawning, he went to the entrance and punched in his special number. The plate-glass door swung open.

"Lucas." The administrative assistant behind the desk greeted him by name each time. She was one of three who worked in this place. Each time he was greeted with a smile, he experienced a beat of relief that Dad was in a good place.

"How's it going?"

"Good as always." The older lady smiled. "They're bringing breakfast around. You're just in time."

He punched in his code at the door to Dad's wing. The sign above read *Late-Stage Care Unit*. At the room, he knocked on the door as he went in. Dad was in a recliner, the one Lucas had grown up with. His gray hair was combed and a towel was draped over his bony knees. "There he is. Up bright and early."

Dad blinked at him. Would he know his own son today? Dad's gaze swung to look back out the window. He wasn't a talker like he used to be. But then, his mind wasn't what it used to be either.

Fucking Alzheimer's.

Lucas rambled, like he usually did, having learned long ago just to lower the floodgates and talk. "So I'm trying to get that old Chevy working again. Hoping to sell it."

"Knock, knock." An aide rolled the food cart into the room, a spring in her step not many people had before noon. "I heard you have a visitor, Herman. I think he's after my job."

Lucas chuckled. It was the same routine, no matter what meal he was here for. The staff had known him for the last eight years. New people came and went, but those who had been here since the beginning, the ones who had encouraged him to visit and trained him on how to act, were like a surrogate family.

More than a *surrogate* family. His aunt ran the place and she was the reason Dad had the care he did. After Mom's sudden death, Aunt Marilyn had swooped in. All of Dad's family had swooped in, but Aunt Marilyn was the only one who'd wanted to help. He'd had little to worry about regarding Dad's care. Just paying for it, though that was more than enough.

The food tray was left for him. Dad couldn't eat by himself, and he got agitated in a group-dining environment. Lucas took the lid off to reveal a bowl of simple oatmeal and apple juice.

"Breakfast of champions," he muttered. Eating was one of the tasks that he used to take for granted but didn't after Dad's decline. "I'm gonna spin you around to eat. When you're done, you can keep looking out the window."

The center had put out bird feeders all over. The residents seemed to enjoy the antics of the squirrels and birds. After he arranged Dad to eat, he dumped a packet of sugar into the oatmeal. Dad ate sweeter food with fewer issues. Thus the oatmeal instead of scrambled eggs.

His only job was to spoon and wait, giving his mind time to wander back to Trina. Why was she living at home? Why did Brayden have to get up early? Trina worked late hours. Was that her normal routine, working late and getting up early?

For someone he used to know so well, he didn't know shit about her now. And that bothered him.

Breakfast was gone. He used the napkin to wipe the corners of Dad's mouth and under his lower lip where some spittle had dribbled out.

"I'll stop in again soon." He said that each time he left. A reassurance. For Dad. For himself. His gaze drifted to the pictures on the wall. The one of him and his parents, two years before the diagnosis. Each time his gaze landed on it, he wondered if there were signs he'd missed, but he'd been a kid. Barely in high school. The world had revolved around him then.

"Love you," he said softly as he walked out.

Walking down the hall, he nodded to other residents' family members. Regulars. The facility was more than a group home, as robust as a nursing home, but it specialized in dementia and head trauma. Injuries, conditions, and chronic diseases that robbed people of their motor or cognitive abilities—or both.

As he neared the staff offices up front, he veered to the right. Maybe Aunt Marilyn was in already. She had no children herself, so she'd likely been here before the day shift arrived and would leave well into the evening shift. Visiting her was a little boost he often needed after being with Dad.

As he approached, Aunt Marilyn's voice rang out. Oh no. She reserved that tone for employees who'd fucked up.

"What we do here is serious. If we invest in an employee

and sponsor their certified nurse's aide training, then we expect dedication. Showing up fifteen minutes late for an interview doesn't show that."

Holy shit, Aunt Marilyn was bringing the hammer down on someone. He felt bad for the poor soul in her office.

"I… I'm sorry. I have no excuse."

His stomach plummeted. Trina was the poor sap? This was her appointment and she'd been late.

If she was interviewing, she had to be looking for a job, a way out of the bar scene. The hours here would be more flexible and compatible with raising a kid.

He widened his path so he could see inside. Trina sat across from Aunt Marilyn's desk. The starkness of his aunt's office cast a pallor across Trina's face. Either that or she was just pale. Her shoulders were hunched and her knuckles were white where she clenched her hands in her lap.

"I think we're done here—"

He rushed to the doorway before Aunt Marilyn finished. "Trina. Why didn't you tell me you had an interview? I wouldn't have kept you up so late."

Trina's eyes were wide when she whipped her head toward the door.

He continued with the crazy idea that sprang into his mind. "Aunt Marilyn, I'm really sorry. Trina was helping me fix up the Chevy. I kept her up late." His aunt's face transformed from stern to serious. She knew how important it was for him to finish that pickup. He switched his attention to Trina. "Didn't want me know who your interview was with? Afraid to abuse my connections?"

Trina's jaw dropped. From her stunned expression, she hadn't connected the dots of who Aunt Marilyn was to him. He hadn't gotten close to his aunt until after Mom had died —then even more so after his divorce.

Marilyn blinked. "I...didn't realize you two knew each other."

"We're—"

Before Trina could tack on *neighbors*, he rushed ahead. "Dating. Trina and I are seeing each other."

CHAPTER 2

The strangest high-pitched whistle filled her brain. He'd just lied to the director of the Quality of Life Center. Not just any lie.

He'd said they were dating.

Trina's gaze flew to the director. Marilyn Peterson was his aunt? There were several Petersons in the area, and she hadn't added two and two.

She needed to correct him. And yet, Director Peterson didn't just work here, she also ran the practical nursing program in town. Getting a job here would boost her chances of getting into the program and getting her LPN. With zero healthcare experience under her belt, she *needed* this job. The center covered the cost of the CNA program while allowing their new hires to work in housekeeping or the kitchen until they were certified. Without it, she couldn't afford to start a new career.

The pay, the shift work, and the potential to work on her bachelor's in nursing via distance learning after getting her LPN would help her not only raise her son, but do adult shit like plan for his college.

With a career in nursing, she could rent an apartment bigger than a six-pack. She could tuck him in at night instead of hiring a teenager and crossing her fingers that a kid not much older than her son wouldn't invite anyone over or take a billion pictures of Brayden and post them online or siphon the tip money she collected in her bedroom drawer.

If she were a nurse, there would be more job opportunities. Shift work was a cuss word for some, but for her and Brayden, it was ideal. She'd worked every weekend and all evenings since he'd been born. They needed a change. *She* needed a change.

"You—you're dating?" Marilyn's gaze jumped between them.

Her phone buzzed in her purse. Trina groaned inwardly. How could one of the most critical days of her life be going so poorly? She'd slept past her alarm. Thankfully, Brayden had woken up early and turned the TV on to blare across the house. Then her ex had berated her for not dropping Brayden off on time, costing her precious minutes. When she'd skidded into the center and seen Director Peterson's disapproving frown, she'd almost cried. And she'd cried herself out years ago.

"We're…" Trina couldn't bring herself to say no. Lucas's guilty ass gave her an out. But she wasn't saved yet. She lifted her gaze to meet his. The man was grinning. His shit-eating smile sparked a forbidden glow in her belly but also sent a flush of heat to her face that had nothing to do with desire.

He was enjoying this.

"Yes, ma'am," he said. "We've known each other forever, but we only started seeing each other recently. This is Davina Hart's daughter."

Marilyn's eyes widened. "Oh. You're…neighbors?"

Trina cringed. Mom and Sarah had been a couple for

almost twenty years. She'd heard it all. Jokes. Ridicule. Blatant hate. Even acceptance.

Talk and speculation had died down over the years, but a tone like Marilyn's often meant rainbow-loving vibes weren't next.

"Yes, we're dating." The words were out of Trina's mouth before she knew it.

Lucas wanted to help her? Well, it was his fault she'd slept late. The sheer delight on Director Peterson's face when he popped in must mean he was close to his aunt.

His brow lifted enough to show his surprise at her willingness to go along. "Catch me outside when you're done, *sweetie*. I'd better leave you two alone."

"How was Herman?" Director Peterson asked before he could leave.

Lucas's dad living here was another reason she'd wanted the job. Herman had been her savior during the rocky years of her parents' marriage—which was every year Dad had been around. Trina could run next door for any meal, any time of the day, and Herman and Barbara would invite her in.

But then Lucas had quit talking to her. Football. Muddin' with Aaron Walker. And once Shaylee had entered his life, Trina doubted he'd realized other girls existed. Her friendship with him had disappeared with their toy trucks and tree forts. No more long afternoons playing in that old shed on his property.

It didn't stop her from wanting to help Herman any way possible, to make sure he was indeed getting the best of care. Not that Director Peterson wasn't already making sure too.

"Dad was good." Lucas wasn't as solemn as she'd expected. He'd dealt with his dad's reality. "Ate like a champ." He leaned in with a wink. "Of course, I always add an extra sugar packet to his oatmeal."

Director Peterson chuckled. "I know you do. That's why I told the kitchen to toss another on there when you're showing up."

Lucas nodded and left. Trina's gaze lingered on the way his hips rolled when he wore his boots. She turned back. The director watched her.

"You and Lucas, huh."

Trina nodded, all the anxiety from earlier rushing back. "He's…changed."

"How so?" The question was calculating. More like a test than an interview. Definitely not idle chitchat.

Since the lie was sizeable, she went for honesty. "We were close as kids, but grew apart. I didn't talk to him much until after his divorce. It's nice to see him…lighter." She'd been about to say happier, but that wasn't quite true. He wasn't the laughing, mischievous kid she'd known.

He'd gotten sloppy drunk in the bar a few times. She'd called him a cab twice. His best friend Aaron had taken his keys the other times.

A ghost of a smile crossed the director's lips. It was the first shadow of approval aimed toward her. "Lighter. That's a good term for it. So, let's get to the interview then. Why do you want to work here?"

Trina had a whole spiel in place. The quality of care, the reputation of the facility, her own strong work ethic, blah, blah, blah. Director Peterson sat behind her desk, her expression passive, her hands folded on the desktop. Imposing. Formidable. Unwilling to deal with any bullshit.

"I want to apply for nursing school. I thought being here, working under you, would be a good way to determine if this really is the career path for me." Her phone buzzed again. She shifted, as if that would hide the noise. Who the hell had to call her at eight thirty in the morning?

The director reclined, her scrutiny uncomfortable. "And

why do you think nursing would be for you if your only job has been in a bar?"

Ask a sixteen-year-old kid what they wanted to be when they grew up, and everybody cheered whatever answer they gave. But ask a grown-up who'd worked her ass off since she could hold a job what she wanted to do with her life? All she got was "are you sure?"

"I really don't know why. I just feel driven to learn about it. But at this stage in my life, I have to be smart. I can't leave high school graduation and go right into college like other students. I have bills. I have a son." *I'm in my thirties, for God's sake.* Thirty-one. She wanted to finish college before her kid did.

"And we'll sponsor your CNA training." The director didn't say it like it was a strike against her.

"And you have a strong reputation for quality care."

The woman narrowed her eyes. Trina wasn't sure what else to say when the director sighed. "Lucas is a reference I can't refuse. When can you start?"

What? As easy as that? All because of Lucas?

Damn that man. How long was she going to have to pretend to date him?

THE WAIT WAS WORTH IT. Lucas stood beside his truck, focused on the center's entrance. How was Trina going to come out? Steaming mad? Triumphant? Sad?

He couldn't do sad. She'd had enough of sad. His intention had been to help. The selfishness was an unfortunate by-product of his haphazard pursuit. Or the cause of it.

Trina burst through the doors, her hips swinging, and her gaze zeroed in on him. The line of her mouth was set like she was in the bar—and dealing with a pushy customer. Or, yeah, like she was dealing with him.

Since she'd been sitting in the hot seat for her interview, he hadn't gotten to see how she'd dressed.

At the bar, she wore jeans that hugged her ass and a tucked-in T-shirt that only accentuated the flare of her hips and her strong shoulders. He admired her shoulders. Not a body part he ever thought he'd fixate on, but here he was, eyeing how today's blousy top hung loose over her slacks. Her frame was powerful. Just like her. They'd been evenly matched as children. Racing horses through the pastures. Climbing the loft in the barn. Skating over frozen stock ponds. Neither one of them had backed down.

That haircut. When he'd first seen her with that style, he'd choked on his drink. The delicate line of her neck offered a hint of the softness he might find if she ever let him close. She was a head shorter than him, but he could easily lean down and nuzzle along her neckline.

She came to a stop in front of him and planted her hands on her hips. "Lucas Herman Peterson, what the hell were you thinking?"

He winced. No one had called him by his full name in years. Mom used to, and not just when she was angry. Shaylee had refused to say his whole name, probably because it would have reminded her of his obligation to his dad. The wince was from the tug of longing that hit him when it rolled off Trina's lips. "I was thinking that you needed help and Aunt Marilyn adores me."

"You shamelessly exploited her feelings."

He lifted a shoulder and gave her the lazy smile that drove her crazy. "She doesn't have kids of her own. I was always her favorite of the nieces and nephews."

Trina's look said she wasn't buying it. Like she could see right through him. Like she knew that Marilyn had become a second mom to him and that, to her, he was a link to her brother. Or more importantly, she sensed that he and Aunt Marilyn had become the biggest sources of support for each other when the whole world had abandoned them.

"I got the job."

A weight rolled off his shoulders. "Really? She was reading you quite the riot act when I walked by."

"She barely interviewed me," Trina said flatly. "Thanks to you. But I'll take whatever advantage I can get."

"Are you still going to be working at Barley 'n' Hops?"

"Not as much. And not a minute too soon. I work tonight, though." A scowl crossed her face. She reached into her pocket for her phone. Her features went tight. "Or maybe not."

"What's going on?"

She cast him a suspicious look. "Nothing."

"If we're dating, I should know."

"We're not dating. We're pretending." She glanced over her shoulder as if Aunt Marilyn would suddenly appear. "Fine. Brayden's dad canceled on me. Again. Brayden was supposed to sleep over because I close tonight."

Her ex. Lucas had wanted to ask her what she'd been thinking when she'd started seeing Paxton Betts. The guy reminded him too much of her dad. Dismissive and insulting behind a polished exterior.

She huffed. "And of course Pax knows how hard it is to get a teenage babysitter in the middle of summer. I should've taken the week off."

"I'll watch him."

Trina snapped her mouth shut.

"I'm serious," he said. "He can come over, or I can go over there. I should go to Davina's. All his toys will be there."

"Lucas, I don't think—"

"Don't you trust me with him?" It was one thing for her to

ignore him while she was working. He'd been admittedly obnoxious. But to not want her kid around him?

"I don't know you. We ran all over the county when we were kids. Then you moved on. Got married to perfect little Shaylee and didn't even say hi when we passed within feet of each other." She pressed her lips together like she'd said too much. "Anyway. If we're fake dating, then I have to shelter him from thinking you're a guy who's coming into our lives."

He considered her statement. They'd grown apart as they'd gotten older. But she'd had her friends and he'd had his. Right? He tried to recall who she'd hung around but couldn't come up with any names.

Shielding Brayden from thinking Lucas was a new father figure was a smart thing to do. When he'd been married, she'd dated his best friend. Aaron had mentioned never being allowed to cross paths with Brayden. Geez, the boy had to have been only three or so then. But if his own father was a flake, he didn't need more guys strolling in and out of his life.

"When we're around him, just friends. We can do that, can't we, Tree-bee?"

"Stop with the nickname."

"It's payback for Lucas Herman." If he pretended his full name irritated him, would she use it more?

Trina looked around the parking lot. Only two rows of cars took up the space. Staff parking was in the back, and unfortunately, the visitor lot was never full. "You can come over around four. I won't be home until after one."

"Who's watching him the rest of the week?"

"Hopefully his dad, but we'll see if he cancels. I'm sure it was daunting to think of taking care of his own son for twenty-four hours. I only work until ten the rest of the week so I can pick him up after. You know, to keep Pax from stressing."

Paxton couldn't take his own son for a week? What a douche. "When do you start here?"

"Not soon enough. Training begins in two weeks, so I have a couple of days of paperwork and videos and orientation. Then I start the CNA course."

"The pay won't be as good as the tips at the bar."

Her expression was pure Trina: mutinous and frustrated. "Small-town bars don't tip shit."

"Not when you're grumpy." He smiled to take the edge off. She knew as well as he did that she was efficient and prompt with her work, but she wasn't flirtatious or tolerant of derogatory behavior. And it cost her money.

"I settled on grumpy after getting my ass slapped a hundred times."

He'd offer to break the arm of anyone who'd tried to touch her without permission, but she'd been handling herself just fine. She might break *his* arm for asking.

"Why here?" He had chores to get home and do. Crops that needed spraying. But she was standing still and talking to him. A scenario he'd been beginning to believe would never happen.

"Your aunt is the nursing school director too. I want to be an LPN."

"Really?"

She folded her arms across her chest. "Why is everyone so surprised?"

"Like you said, we don't know each other. You've been in food service since you were old enough to work."

"Can't a girl change careers without the world having to end first?"

"Yes, she can." Except Trina didn't change.

His answer was enough to soften her. "Benefits. Flexibility. More pay. Interest." Her lower lip stuck out in a near pout and it was the cutest thing he'd ever seen. "Maybe I saw a few shows and thought it looked like fun."

He laughed. "Getting your career ideas from Netflix?"

She glared at him, her arms folding tighter. "It was on cable. One of those reality shows." Her phone buzzed again. She dropped her arms and he *did not* like the frown on her face one bit. "I'd better get going before Pax comes up with more ailments that prevent him from caring for his child."

"Oh, you can't just leave." He sauntered closer to her. "Aunt Marilyn's office is right there. She might be watching us. A goodbye kiss is probably expected between two people who are dating."

She glared at him as he leaned closer. He wasn't going to push it, but he wasn't going to let the opportunity slide. She'd ignored him for too long.

Pressing his lips against hers, he didn't take it further. Just a simple molding of his lips to hers. A perfect fit. She tensed her mouth, returning his kiss only briefly.

He took his time drawing back and slowly opened his eyes to stare into the sparkling mix of green and brown in her irises. Wariness hovered in their depths.

He tried to swallow back the swell of emotion that caught him by surprise. The reminder that he hadn't kissed anyone for…years. The choking resentment of being cheated on by the woman he'd thought he'd spend the rest of his life with. The way he *wanted* to want more—in his personal life, in the career that had been decided for him after his dad's diagnosis —but he didn't dare hope. Life had shown him he didn't deserve more.

He cleared his throat and averted his gaze. "See you at four, Trina." When he got into his truck, he couldn't look back at her. That one kiss had tugged a string that threatened to unravel all the things he told himself to get through life.

CHAPTER 3

"So, um, my friend Lucas is coming over to watch you tonight." Trina wrinkled her nose. Her casual tone was a fail, but her son wasn't paying attention.

Brayden crouched by his Beyblade, setting up the next battle. "Lucas? Nana and Gramma's neighbor?"

"You know him?" She'd been avoiding Lucas. How could Brayden know him?

He lifted a bony shoulder and concentrated on his task. "He helps them out. Always waves at me and stuff."

"Uh-huh." She'd spent the whole day planning how to broach this subject. Guys were never in her home if Brayden might see them. But no, this was good. Brayden knew Lucas. To him, Lucas was a neighbor. That was all.

Then why did her lips still tingle? And why were her thoughts returning to last night and how good Lucas's ass looked in his jeans?

She pressed her hand to her belly. After years of leaving Brayden with sitters, she shouldn't be nervous.

"How's lasagna sound for supper?" she called as she went

into the kitchen. The meal was frozen solid and would take a good two hours to cook. Lucas wouldn't have to do a thing.

Her gaze strayed to the clock. Time was moving so slow. Not that she was looking forward to seeing Lucas. And not after that chaste, but unsettling kiss. Had it been her imagination, or had he changed after? Had he been disappointed? Just messing with her?

Of course he'd been messing with her.

Yet she'd agreed to it.

"Does Lucas like lasagna?" Brayden hollered from the other room.

She stopped and spun around. He'd never asked about the preferences of previous sitters. "I...don't know. Doesn't everyone?"

"Maybe breadsticks too?"

"They're in the freezer if he wants to cook them."

A knock on the door made her jump. Already?

No, he was early.

"Come in!" Brayden scrambled off the floor and sprinted for the door.

She watched, unable to keep her jaw from hanging open as Brayden skidded to a stop in front of the old door off the kitchen. Lucas stepped inside. Her heart skipped a beat, then stuttered as Lucas held his fist out. Brayden bumped his fist against it and they both did the boom fingers.

When the hell...?

She managed to keep her astonishment out of her voice. "Brayden, you're supposed to see who's at the door before you let them in."

"I knew it was Lucas." Brayden grabbed the man's hand and towed him into the living room. Like an excited little tugboat and a powerful freighter. "Come on, I want to show you my battle."

"Not so fast, kiddo. I need to talk to Lucas first." The

mom in her should be delighted at her son's reaction. But her end goal wasn't to live with her moms the rest of her life. What happened when she moved out of this house?

"Fine." He dropped Lucas's hand and disappeared into the living room. When she returned her attention to the perplexing man in the kitchen, a flush crawled up her neck. He was watching her, that aggravating twinkle in his eyes.

"We're buds," he said as if that explained everything.

"You two certainly seem familiar."

"He plays outside a lot when your moms are out working. And I've helped work cattle a few times when you were busy."

Yes, because she'd done a stellar job of avoiding him. Though she'd mostly been avoiding his perfect ex-wife when Shaylee had lived next door. Her patronizing smile and less-than-subtle eye rolls when she thought no one was looking had made it too tempting to punch her. Or punch Lucas for not realizing how poorly they fit together in the first place.

"I was glad they started asking me." He took his cap off and hung it on the peg by the door. How comfortable was he in this place? "I kept offering, and Sarah is always willing to haul grain."

"Your ex scared them away."

He grimaced, and a flash of guilt passed through her. "Shaylee wasn't the friendliest neighbor." He let out a long exhale. "She hated the farmer's life, and I think she was afraid I'd take up ranching, too, and be busy all year long."

"Did you want to?"

"Hell, yeah. I could use the money." He clamped his lips shut like he'd said too much. "So what's the plan for tonight? Food allergies? Screen-time limits? Any details I need to know?"

He sounded like he'd done some research before coming over. She wanted to go back and learn why he'd changed the subject so quickly. "He can watch a show or two later. Eight o'clock bedtime in the summer. No allergies yet, but he's worried you might not like lasagna."

"Aw, he's always so sweet." The way Lucas beamed when he talked about Brayden robbed her of words. Her silence pushed past uncomfortable. He mumbled, "I like kids."

It hit her. He'd wanted kids. He was, what, thirty-two? No, he was two years older than her. Thirty-three. He'd been married, hoping for the whole package, and now he was alone. Brayden might've been unplanned and his arrival had signaled the end of an unstable relationship, but she couldn't imagine the last seven years without him.

"Well, he likes you," she said, then rattled off instructions for the meal and bedtime routine. "Oh, and Mom and Sarah might call to chat with him." They hadn't given up their landline, but they probably had Lucas's number. Which she also needed. "What's your phone number?"

His lopsided grin was back as he dragged out his phone. "What are you going to put me under as a contact?" Without asking, she knew he was punching in *Tree-bee*.

"'The dick next door.' Don't put Tree-bee. It sounds like I'm a bug." And reminded her of how much fun they used to have. Sometimes she wondered if that was the last time she'd been carefree.

His deep laugh rumbled too close to parts she didn't want to acknowledge around him. "'The rancher next door'? Is that better?"

"Hardly." She'd talked with her moms. When they were done, Trina might get the ranch. Or sell. Whatever worked for her life. And the way Brayden talked, he was going to take over as soon as he got his own horse. "I'll put 'farmer next door' for you. Satisfied?"

He lowered his voice and it did disturbing things to her belly. "Oh, honey. I'm nowhere near satisfied."

"Get used to it." She smiled sweetly and went to say goodbye to Brayden.

∼

Either he was dreaming, or Trina was calling his name. She never talked to him.

He peeled his eyes open. The faint light from the old creamer jug lamp on the end table cast its dull glow over Trina. She was perched on the end of the coffee table in front of the sofa he'd fallen asleep on.

"Shit." He sat up. "Sorry." His knees were beside her, but she didn't scoot away. She would've fallen off the side, but he'd take what he could get.

"No worries. I already checked on Brayden." She glanced around the living room.

He and Brayden had played a cleaning game before bed. The little guy had picked up all his toys out here and in his bedroom. For payment, Lucas had read for forty-five minutes straight. They might've missed the eight o'clock curfew, but not by much.

"How'd it go?" she asked.

"Good." He let out a chuckle. "That kid has an imagination and enough energy to take over the world."

Trina's smile was one of the most genuine he'd seen in a long time. "He's great. Sometimes, I wonder if an alien invaded Pax's body and inseminated me." A light blush stained her cheeks. Had she never joked about that before?

"What was with you and Paxton anyway?"

He didn't expect her to answer, but the shadows of the living room added to the illusion that this was a safe space, a place to confess anything.

Trina brushed a hand over her short spikes. She didn't do much to her hair before work, just enough to lift the few inches off her forehead. "He was new to town. At the time he was going to buy Barley 'n' Hops, but the deal fell through. That should've been the first sign. He gave me some bullshit reason that made it sound like the other party had left Pax hanging, but I'm sure it was his fault. He was a trust-fund baby, you know."

"No. But it fits."

"That stereotype was made for him. He's met someone new. She comes first. Even before his kid. And as he ages, I think the stress of life gets to him. Like all the questions Brayden asks. The kid's mind doesn't shut off and it over-whelms his dad." She gripped the edge of the coffee table until her knuckles turned white.

Did she ever talk to anyone about it? He never saw her out. When he did, she was working.

When her dad had left, they'd ridden horses to one of the many rock piles on his property, climbed to the top, and talked. It never started out with how her dad had disap-pointed her, or the way he'd run her down and left her mom to do everything. But eventually, they got there. Then it'd turn to how her dad had quit talking to her when she'd accepted Sarah into her life. The man couldn't get over his humiliation that not only had his wife moved on, but she'd done it with a woman. And not only had she done it with a woman, but with a partner who refused to let Davina put up with one more ounce of Nathan Hart's verbal abuse.

Then life was good and he and Trina had drifted apart. Then his life wasn't good anymore and he'd had no one. Why'd he never asked Trina to go riding again so they could talk?

Why had they drifted apart?

He had so many questions, just like Brayden. "His ques-tions definitely work my brain. Shit I'd never think to ponder."

Trina's hold on the table loosened and color flooded back into her hand. "He's like a philosopher packed into a Power Ranger's body."

An accurate description. "How was work?"

She lifted a shoulder. "It's never too busy on a Monday. I doubt I made even fifty in tips. But that's okay. There's a bachelorette Friday that I have to work." Her eyes darkened and her mouth puckered like he'd shoved a lemon wedge into it. "I hate working bachelor and bachelorette parties."

"Don't they buy a ton of booze and tip big?" His own had been…rowdy. He'd been all of twenty-one, with a ton of loans under his belt and poor ideas about how to use the money. Shaylee had encouraged every poor decision.

"They leave a mess, get sloppy drunk, and destroy the restrooms. I don't know how many times I've had to use my tips to cover their stiffed bills."

"What? That's crazy." He wanted names. Details. He'd hunt them down, no matter when it had happened. "How is that legal?"

"We're paid minimum wage, and I guess since our paycheck isn't affected, they can order us to pay in our tip money. Something about it being our fault that we didn't collect, I dunno. I don't want to get fired and I can't afford to sue, so now, I stand there until I see the money."

"Who the fuck has left you with their tab?"

She rolled her eyes toward him, her gaze warning him that he wouldn't like her answer. "You. And Shaylee."

He must look like a fish stranded on shore. His eyes were wide, his mouth working.

She nodded and filled in. "You and Aaron took care of your parts, but remember Noble was one of your grooms-men? He was too drunk and I made him call a cab. He refused to pay me since he was pissed that I'd kicked him out."

Lucas shook his head. He didn't remember any of that. But Noble hadn't been the only one shit-faced. "Why didn't you tell me?"

"It was your bachelor party. I didn't really want to deal with the wrath of you or your groomsmen."

"We wouldn't have done that." From the lifting of her brows, she didn't agree. "What about Shaylee?" Her party had been the same night, but they'd had it all planned out so they wouldn't cross paths.

"I almost got fired." Her jaw was rigid and he could almost hear her teeth grinding together. "Her whole party giggled as they left. I ran out to the parking lot, but they pretended not to hear me."

"That…" The sad fact that he'd married someone so self-centered was still sinking in. "I shouldn't be shocked. I'm sorry. How much do I owe you?"

Trina stared at him for a heartbeat. "Why would you— That was years ago."

"How much?"

She tilted her head. "Are you telling me that you're able to dig out a few hundred dollars right now and pay me back?"

Ouch. Hundreds? He was hoping to sell his old truck for a few grand if he could actually get it running decently, but that money was supposed to go to the center. Then he'd be in the middle of harvest and filling his November contract. He'd already taken an advance on the corn and that money would get him through the summer. But until he delivered, he wouldn't get paid the rest.

"It was a long time ago and it's done." She slid to the end of the table and started to stand.

He caught her arm. "Why didn't you tell me? I would've covered it." A lot easier then than now. Back then he'd thought loans would bail him out, and maybe they would've if he hadn't been young and stupid about money.

Her body was primed to run. She vibrated under his grip. "We weren't exactly talking."

"And why is that?"

"You hit puberty and being friends with a girl wasn't cool?"

He scoffed. "I wasn't that shallow." There was that look again. The one she gave him in the bar when she didn't want to deal with him. "I wasn't."

"Whatever. It was a long time ago."

"But here we are." She tensed again, her gaze dropping to where his hand was circled around her wrist. He tempted fate and stroked her soft skin with his thumb. She jerked like he'd grabbed her ass. He released her.

She rose and cleared some space between them, heading for the door. "I'll pay you what I usually pay the sitter, if that's okay." She reached into her pocket and counted out a small amount of tip money.

"You think after what you told me that I'm going to take money?" He waited for her to look at him, struggling not to be insulted. "Besides, I wouldn't take money anyway. Playing Beyblasters is the most fun I've had in a while."

The corner of her mouth hitched up. "Beyblades."

"Well, they make blasting noises." He went to the door, passing close enough to her to make his hand tingle. Her skin was enticingly soft. "You know where to find me if Pax flakes again."

"Thank you." She dropped her gaze, and her expression wavered enough to reveal staggering vulnerability. In the next blink it was gone and tough Trina was back.

"No problem. It's what neighbors do." He stepped outside into the night. Slapping mosquitoes, he walked home. To his quiet house. He didn't want Pax to keep letting Brayden and Trina down, yet he hoped for another night like this. He hadn't lied. It was the best he'd had in a long time.

CHAPTER 4

Trina eyed the group tucked into the corner of the bar. The women laughed and drank. All except one. She sipped her cranberry spritzer. To the untrained eye, it looked like a fancy cocktail. But since Trina had served Shaylee, she knew there was nothing but juice and mineral water in the glass.

How fortuitous. She'd just relived the humiliation that was Shaylee Peterson's first bachelorette party and here she was, on her second. Sort of. It was an engagement party.

Did Lucas know that his ex was engaged to the dentist she'd been having an affair with?

Did he suspect she was pregnant like Trina did? A nonalcoholic drink for a soon-to-be bride? Not to mention the *don't you dare say a damn thing* look Shaylee had shot her when she'd ordered.

Trina got only a small amount of satisfaction when she refused their request after delivering drinks.

Can't we start a tab?

Nope. They'd painfully counted out their cash and given her a small enough tip to be insulting, but at least Trina wasn't going to lose it all paying for drinks she hadn't enjoyed.

Shaylee had a veil on, the rest of her outfit so much different than last time. Trina shouldn't remember in vivid detail the short skirt and corset top Shaylee had worn at her first bachelorette party. Tonight, she was in skinny jeans, flats, and a flowy, empire-waisted top. Not maternity wear, but forgiving, for those early months when the first few pounds felt like eighty.

Trina grabbed a rag and scrubbed the bar. This was a momentary lull in her Friday shift, but she'd be done in an hour, at ten. Missing the later hours meant missing the best tips. It also meant missing the rowdiest of behavior, the cops she had to call way too often, and the vomit in the bathroom.

Putting off checking on the bachelorette crowd as long as she could, she dropped a load of dirty glasses in the wash bin and spun around.

A surprised sound choked off in her throat. "Shaylee." The dainty woman tapped her fingers at the bar, but she didn't look annoyed. Just nervous. "I was just coming to check on your table. What can I get you?"

"Another cranberry spritzer." Her ruby lips pursed.

Trina squatted to grab the cranberry juice out of the mini fridge.

When she rose, Shaylee was watching her. "Have you seen Lucas lately?"

She busied herself with mixing juice and seltzer water.

Not only had she seen Lucas recently, he was at her house right now. Pax had hung in there for the rest of the week, but tonight he'd claimed his girlfriend wanted to head out of town to see her parents. Since the girlfriend was probably paying, Pax wanted to go. He hadn't said as much, but since Trina had given up the fight for child support years ago, she knew. If she pushed harder, she was afraid Pax would blow town and refuse to be in Brayden's life at all, and she'd lose what little help he offered.

"Lucas? Not a lot. It's summer. I'm sure he's busy, right?" As if Shaylee had ever been invested in farm life. Did she even know when the crops were planted?

"Yeah." Shaylee looked away but not toward her group of friends. "I thought I heard you moved back home."

"I did." Trina slid the drink across the counter. "Five dollars."

Shaylee dug a five out of her pocket and dropped it on the table. No extra. That would be the theme of taking care of that crowd. "If you see him, can you tell him to call me?"

Why the hell would she be a go-between? "Sure. Enjoy your *juice*."

Shaylee's shoulders stiffened but she walked away.

That was a little catty, but Trina couldn't help it. She didn't want to do Shaylee's dirty work. Unless the woman was calling to apologize, she was more likely to heap angst onto Lucas's plate. But Trina wasn't going to act like she was jealous and keep tonight to herself. Well, the request, not the pregnancy suspicions. As much as Lucas seemed to genuinely enjoy her son, she couldn't escape feeling like this news would devastate him. Shaylee had not only moved on from their marriage, but she was starting the family Lucas had wanted.

Business picked up for the rest of the shift. Taking her waitress apron off, she folded it neatly and tucked it in her cubby. Her excitement to return home and see how the boys were doing dimmed under the shadow of the "Shaylee wants to talk to you" message.

Hadn't the woman tried calling? Lucas didn't seem like a guy who'd change his number out of spite. But he *did* seem like a guy who'd take his wife back.

Was that why she hated passing along the message? No,

she was irritated because Lucas's drama was none of her business. And because they'd been friends once and she didn't want to see him hurt.

When she pulled into her driveway, the two-story farmhouse was dark. Brayden's night-light cast a faint glow against the not-quite-set summer sun. She parked on the gravel pad, not using the garage since it was summer and Mom and Sarah didn't use garage door remotes for the old, heavy doors.

Inside, she toed her shoes off. Coming home when Lucas watched Brayden was different than coming home to a sitter. Her work wasn't done yet when she had to pay a kid and worry about that kid driving home in the dark. Not only did Lucas refuse her money, he only had to walk across the yard and around the anorexic row of trees to his own property.

Tinny voices came from the TV. He was reclined on the couch, his feet crossed on the coffee table, his hat pushed back. With his arms folded across his chest and his head resting on the cushions, he barely looked awake.

But he was. "How was the night?"

She entered the living room far enough to see that the news was on. Getting too close to him was a bad idea. When he'd clasped her wrist the other night, she hadn't wanted him to let go. "Shouldn't I be asking you that?"

"Getting a kid to sleep when the sun's out is no joke."

She barked out a laugh. "It would be worse if he weren't an early bird."

"That has to be hard when you work nights."

"That should change soon." She crossed to the couch, not knowing when she'd decided that sitting on the same piece of furniture would be a better idea. Perhaps the conversational topic had demolished her hesitation. "Listen, Shaylee was in tonight."

Lucas's attention went back to the TV. "Oh yeah."

"She's getting married."

He nodded, the move knocking his cap off-kilter. Sweeping it off his head, he tossed it onto the coffee table. "I heard." He looked at her. "She texted me."

His flat tone must be all the enthusiasm he could summon for his ex-wife. She didn't blame him. "She, uh, wants you to call her?"

An incredulous look darkened his brown eyes. "She asked you to tell me that?"

Trina nodded. "She heard I'd moved back home. My personal life seems to get talked about around town. I guess it's news."

"Did she say why?"

The cranberry spritzer ran through her mind. "No."

Lucas grunted. "I haven't been answering her calls."

"You rebel, you." She kept the astonishment out of her face. Lucas had been like a puppy dog lapping at Shaylee's heels. Anyone Shaylee picked would've been the same. She'd been voted Best Personality. Bubbly. Pretty. Desired by every guy within five years of her age, and envied by her peers. And Shaylee had known how to pick the one man who'd turn himself inside out for her.

He shot her a playful glare. "Believe me, it's not easy. When I used to miss a call..." Shaking himself, he lifted his feet down and sat forward, his elbows on his knees. He should look as out of place as a bull in the heifer pasture, but he fit. And she wasn't a heifer. "You're off all weekend?"

Her stomach fluttered like it had in the days when she wanted a guy she was interested in to ask her out. When was the last time that had happened? Lately, if she went home with a guy, or invited him over while Brayden was asleep and clueless, it was out of boredom. Vibrators were nice and all, but they weren't what she preferred.

"No work, but I have a ton of boxes in the shed to go

through before they get mouse infested. I can't believe how much of Brayden's stuff I kept."

"Not planning any more kids?"

"Not in the near future." She'd never had a reason to think about more kids. After the shock of Brayden, she'd started on birth control and none of her dates had made her think beyond a hookup to breakfast, much less expanding her family. "Besides, he's seven. With how fast kid stuff changes, who knows what'll be recalled or expired by the time I'm in a place to have more."

"I wouldn't know anything about that." His gaze dropped. "I wanted, like, three kids. Shaylee said we'd have no more than two—more than one so they could keep each other company. But she never wanted to discuss when. I was starting to wonder if I'd have to change my outlook on family life. I don't know if she ever wanted kids."

Trina chewed the inside of her lip. If she knew for sure, maybe she'd spill the secret. But Shaylee's baby status was nothing but speculation.

He grabbed his cap but didn't stand. "Send Brayden over if you need a break. Or you both can come over. I can grill or something."

Since Brayden had talked nonstop about getting to play with Lucas tonight, she didn't want to get her son's hopes up that Lucas was a long-term prospect. "Mom and Sarah are coming home tomorrow." As if that would explain why she couldn't come over.

He nodded, but his shoulders hung an inch lower than before. When had annoying Lucas turned into the guy who didn't pester her? "Is that all you're going to do?" she snapped.

His brows popped up. "S'cuse me?"

She waved her hand at him. "Where's the guy who'd make some caustic remark about my hair? Or how long I took to get you a refill? Where's the guy that played his music loud when he damn well knew I was trying to sleep?"

A slow smile crept over his face. "That guy's kind of a dick."

"But he's the dick I grew up with. I kind of liked that guy."

"What about now?" His voice had dropped and his eyelids were hooded. Was he leaning closer? Or was she?

The air charged between them. Electricity skittered over her skin. "I still find him annoying. But I think he has a warm, squishy center."

"Oh, honey," he drawled. "My center isn't squishy."

How had he gone from such a depressing conversation to this? No doubt Shaylee wanted to tell him in person that she was getting married to Dr. Do-Me. If Lucas wanted to test whether he'd moved on or not, that'd do it.

But at the moment, he didn't care who she married. His lips were inches from Trina's and he wasn't stopping.

And she wasn't halting him.

Like in the parking lot outside of the center, when his mouth had landed on hers, he couldn't believe how well they fit. He pressed her back against the cushioned arm of the floral-patterned couch. He could've cheered when her arms snaked around his neck. Using his to keep from bending her backward until they both spilled over the edge, he stayed close enough to savor the length of her strong body against his.

When she opened her mouth for him, he sank down a little farther. Sweeping his tongue inside the warm depths of her mouth, he couldn't shut his mind off. He was kissing Trina. The girl next door. Had all her ballbusting in the bar been a show?

His had been. She was right. He had the squishiest of centers. His ex-wife had exploited that.

But he hadn't been lying. Right now, there was nothing soft or malleable behind the fly of his jeans.

A whimper escaped Trina as their tongues tangled. It was the most feminine sound he'd ever heard her make. Could he make her do it again? She widened her legs, wrestling them out from under him until he was cradled against her. He rocked against her before he could ask himself if it was going too far for a make-out session.

When she thrust up to meet him, he would've grinned if his tongue wasn't tasting everything she had to offer. Well—not everything. The throbbing of his erection increased at the thought of getting her pants off. What did his Trina have to offer?

She curled her hands into the back of his shirt and fisted as she undulated against him, needy and straining for what *he* could offer. He'd never thought he had much, but tonight he'd give it his best shot.

They both slid down the couch until they were prone across it. Her legs wrapped around him, and his left leg hung down to the floor, keeping him from crushing her.

How far should he go? God, this wasn't his area of expertise. He was used to being ordered around in bed. His mind regressed until he thought in terms of bases. They were at first. Second was what again? Up the shirt. Okay, he could follow that as a guide.

Of course he could! This wasn't the transactional sex he'd had before. *You didn't take the garbage out, so no sex tonight. I had to work all day.* Because somehow, his work wasn't as important. *I'm really tired, just do your thing. I don't need to get off.* As if he could enjoy sex with a limp partner.

I don't even know why you like going down on me. Isn't it gross? I know I don't like doing it.

His blood supply threatened to abandon his cock. He banned all memories of his past sex life and concentrated on here and now, though it was harder than it ought to be. All the ways he'd disappointed Shaylee rang in his head.

Then Trina stroked herself against his raging erection. She wasn't a liar. If she didn't like what he was doing, she'd let him know. He put more force into the rock of his hips.

She broke away from his mouth to hiss, "Yes."

Bolstered by her reaction, he tunneled his hand under her already bunched up shirt. The slide down the couch had benefitted him greatly. Her breasts were a perfect fit for his palm. He wanted to massage them, learn what she liked, roll the nipple between his thumb and finger, suck the peak into his mouth… But first, the bra. Those things were like Sudoku puzzles. How the hell did they work? He'd never figured either one out.

Instead, he yanked the cup down. Her nipple brushed his fingers as it popped free. The groan that came from her was enough to keep him hard for weeks. Hell, the last few minutes would fuel his lonely shower strokes for years to come.

Nuzzling her neck, he kissed down to her collarbone and relished how she responded. Arching into him, lengthening her neck, rolling up into him.

Enough of this. She *needed*. And he couldn't let her go without.

Adjusting his position to stroke down her stomach, he was stunned that she let him. The pants and gasps escaping her were unmistakable feedback that she wanted this, and it wasn't until now that he realized how he hadn't had that. Ever.

It took a few attempts to get under her jeans. He almost gave up. Add one more strike against him: he literally couldn't get into her pants. It didn't help that they were rubbing against each other, but if he were better at this, his hand would be on her by now.

With a frustrated growl, she flipped open her pants and rocked into him. He slid his hand closer to the furnace of her center, and she widened her legs.

Oh God. This was happening. He was going for it and she was letting him. This was Trina, his prickly neighbor who had ignored him for years.

And what did he have to offer her?

Light bled through his closed eyelids. Trina gasped and jerked upright, shoving him backward. He scrambled to the far corner of the couch as she swung her legs down and yanked her shirt over her gaping jeans. Her cheeks were bright red and her short hair was mussed, softening the angles of her face.

His brain finally registered that the hallway light had flipped on. Hopefully from the top of the stairs and not the bottom.

That was the fastest his libido had been killed and that was saying a lot. When he'd been married, Shaylee had been an expert at nailing him with mood-killing criticisms.

"What's up, bud?" Trina called, avoiding looking in his direction.

"Oh, you're home." Brayden hit the bottom of the stairs. "I need some water." He waved on his way past. Lucas gave him a smile and returned the wave, like he and Trina had been hanging out on opposite ends of the couch this whole time. Brayden disappeared into the kitchen.

Lucas chanced a glance at Trina. Her body was rigid and she stared at the floor in front of her.

A minute later, the boy wandered out of the kitchen toward the stairs, rubbing his eyes. "Night."

"Night," he and Trina said at the same time.

Once the hallway light shut off, he let out a long breath.

Trina rubbed her face. "You need to go home."

"I'm sorry. I shouldn't have— You trusted me to babysit and I— I'm sorry."

She stared at him. "As much as I want to blame you, I was all for it. You didn't hear me say no for a reason."

He stared at her. Had he heard right?

"I like sex. But this could get complicated."

"Yeah." It didn't feel complicated. He liked her kid. She wasn't a newb about country life. Checking mousetraps, hunting down wasp nests, and tripping over the kills the barn cats left on the walking path wouldn't faze her. But he was who he was and he couldn't change it. Lord knew he'd tried and ended up divorced anyway. "And your moms come home soon."

The corner of her mouth hitched up. "I always liked that about you."

"What?" It'd be nice to hear something good about himself for once.

"My moms. The way you say it. You accepted Sarah better than anyone."

"I saw how she treated you and Davina. They're good neighbors." The best. He would've been bankrupt without their help. He huffed out a quiet laugh. "Last winter, I got the skid steer stuck and Sarah pulled me out, and I have a freezer full of prime cuts because I gave your mom the keys to my tractor when the transmission went out on theirs last fall."

"That was expensive. I was worried they wouldn't be able to afford this vacation."

"I have a buddy who's a mechanic. Not for tractors, but since he's been ranching, he's adapted."

Trina cocked her head. "Jesse Rodriguez, right? He charged them half the price and I think that was only because they refused to let him do it for free. You hooked them up? Thank you."

"Anytime." He rose before the conversation could get awkward or return to what a bad idea making out had been. His ego could take it, but it didn't mean he had to. "And I mean it. You need a sitter, or a hand around here, call. I have some uses."

"You turned out to be a pretty good guy, Lucas Herman Peterson."

He smiled as he walked out the door, liking her comment way too much. "Back atcha, Tree-bee."

Two freaking weeks had gone by since that night on the couch with Lucas. Trina stifled a yawn. The classroom portion of her CNA training didn't last long, but she'd worked the bar last night—extra cash while Mom and Sarah were around to help out.

The course was held at the local community college. She'd been able to get her hands on materials she'd use if she got accepted for her LPN. Too bad she hadn't had her shit together last year to apply or she could be starting this fall. But until she'd ridden out her lease, she couldn't have afforded tuition. Moving home had freed up half her paycheck. Brayden was getting older and she hadn't saved much for his school. And Pax... The man blew through money and whined that it was everyone else's fault that they expected him to adult.

Her phone buzzed. It was nestled in the pocket of her scrubs. She didn't look at it until her break. Once in the hall-way, she veered toward the restrooms, waiting until she was tucked behind a stall to look. Director Peterson.

Stop by my office when class is over.

Was she in trouble? Had the woman discovered that she and Lucas weren't dating?

Trina squirmed through the rest of class and practicals and hightailed it to the center when they were dismissed.

The director was in her office, intent on her computer screen. Trina knocked. The urge to run and hide was stronger than she cared to admit.

Director Peterson looked over her glasses at Trina. Her face gave nothing away. "Come in. Have a seat."

Trina sat, her back ramrod straight, her hands on the armrests.

The other woman pushed her reading glasses up and faced her. "What do you think of everything so far?"

"Good." Realizing her usual curt answers weren't useful in this situation, she elaborated. "I like learning something new."

The course was fascinating. She'd tapped into an unknown-to-her world and she was hungry for knowledge. But this was just the beginning of her journey. She didn't want to get her hopes too high only to watch them plummet when life interfered.

"Good." The director's serious expression didn't crack. "I like to check in periodically because it can be shocking. If not in the classroom, then when you're here, confronted with a combative patient or diaper changing an adult."

"I'm sure there will be moments of adjustment." Trina swallowed, willing herself to shut up but her pride wouldn't let her. "But both situations aren't unfamiliar to me. I mean, in the bar, I call the police. Here I'd call for another aide or nurse. But as far as human waste, I've had to clean a lot."

Director Peterson frowned. Did she disapprove of the behavior or her old job? "It wouldn't be occasional. Bathing, changing, and cleaning accidents will be your job."

Trina nodded, firm in her resolve. "Director Peterson, I'd

rather help people who need it than someone who laughs about getting so drunk they puked all over the floor and don't even give a second thought to who cleaned it up."

It must've been the right thing to say. The director nodded like she understood exactly what drove Trina to want to give back to the world. "You see some miracles happen within these walls and you see heartbreak. Sometimes in the same day. So I'm going to touch base during the next few weeks. The families here deserve the best care, but I don't want my employees miserable. And please, call me Marilyn. 'Director Peterson' is a little too formal for our cozy facility."

"Thank you." She left the office but didn't head toward the exit. She paused outside of Director—*Marilyn's* view and glanced down the hall. During her tour, she'd seen where Herman's room was—the big bear of a man with a boisterous laugh who used to keep his beer fridge stocked with Minute Maid lemonade. She'd never visited him. He'd been at Barbara's funeral, but so had the whole town, and it wasn't like she'd stayed to socialize afterward.

Spinning on her heel, she found his room and tapped lightly on the door. The supervisor who'd done her tour had given her a quick rundown on all the patients. Herman could follow simple commands, even sit in a chair, but he couldn't care for himself or hold a conversation. His impressive strength was draining at a rapid rate, but for the most part he was comfortable.

Her heart wrenched when she entered. Herman hadn't acknowledged her knock. The room was dim but the blinds were cracked. His window faced the courtyard.

He was nothing like the Mack truck of man she'd known. His head stooped on his neck and his arms were less than half the size they used to be. Her eyes burned, but she would not cry in front of him. His quiet world didn't need her blustering.

"Hi, Herman," she said quietly. Her supervisor had told her to talk conversationally and that Herman was one of the residents who seemed to like being talked to regularly. "It's Trina Hart. I grew up by your farm."

Her gaze strayed to the wall over his bed where photos were lined up. He'd been here for eight years, but he and Barbara had moved into town shortly after Lucas graduated. Trina hadn't known then, but a few years later, Mom had said it was because Herman had Alzheimer's and senior living was easier for both of the Petersons. Trina hadn't been his neighbor for nearly half her life.

She cleared her throat and tiptoed in. "Lucas's friend. I haven't seen you in a while."

It was odd, being the one to do all the talking. Everyone joked that a bartender's skills included listening and they weren't wrong. There was no reason to talk to anyone who wasn't going to stick around or who'd eventually let her down, and that went beyond just customers.

"I'm going to be working here, so you should see more of me. Um…" What else did she talk about? "Oh, I have a son. Can you imagine? Me, a mom? But he's a good kid. He's seven, and…"

A nurse strode in. Her eyes lit up as she recognized Trina from her rounds of introductions. "I didn't realize you knew Herman here." She held a pill cup in her left hand. It was time for Herman's meds.

Trina was about to answer when a familiar voice broke in. "Trina and Dad go way back." Lucas entered, a smile on his face, but his eyes were contemplative as he looked at her.

"Lucas." Did that breathy sound come from her? She knew what was to blame. The second he walked in, her traitorous body remembered how well he could stroke her in all the right places even with all their clothes on. Her subconscious desperately wanted to know what he could do without a stitch of fabric between them—and without children around to interrupt.

Still not the place to be lusting over an incident that shouldn't have happened.

The nurse busied herself at Herman's side. "How far is way back?" Stella looked over her shoulder as she held the cup of water at Herman's mouth.

"We grew up together." Trina's gaze shifted to Lucas. He stood with his thumbs hooked in his front pockets. Not the Lucas she was used to. He was fluid, easygoing even when he was upset that she was ignoring him. "Neighbors," she finished lamely.

Stella nodded. "Ah, right. That makes sense now. Didn't I hear you two are dating?"

A smirk appeared on Lucas's face. "Aunt Marilyn must've let it slip."

Did everyone know she'd gotten the job because of him?

"What do you think, Herman?" Stella smiled at Herman. "Your son's kind of a catch." She winked toward them.

Lucas's expression drained of humor.

"He sure is," Trina agreed. Stella giggled and Lucas jerked. Yeah, it was the last thing she'd expected to say too. But it was for his dad's benefit. Totally.

"I'll leave you be with your visitors," Stella said to Herman. "But I'll see you later tonight." When Stella left, she swung the door shut behind her.

Lucas's attention was on her. She couldn't read his expression. "Nice of you to stop by."

"I should've done it a long time ago." Feeling like an intruder, she got up. "I wanted to stop and say hi before I started officially working here."

Lucas's gaze strayed to his dad. Herman stared out the

window. Stella had said she'd be back and it was likely to reposition him to prevent bedsores.

During her tour, the supervisor had rattled off other information about all the patients. She'd said that Lucas came nearly every day.

"I'll let you visit." She looked over her shoulder and spoke to Herman. "It was nice to see you again. I feel the need to stop and grab a case of lemonade before I go home."

Herman looked at her. Same eyes, but so very different. She summoned a smile.

"I'll be right back, Dad." Lucas followed her out.

"You don't have to—"

"I've got all night, Trina." They walked along the hallway. Savory smells floated down the hallway. Dinner would be getting served soon. Roast beef and mashed potatoes. A heavy dinner for a hot day, but within these walls the weather was always the same.

As they made the last turn to the exit, Marilyn darted out of her office and into their path.

"I was hoping to catch you." She spoke to Lucas but smiled at Trina. A much different reception than their first meeting. In her hands was a narrow strip of paper. "Do either of you eat at Tyler's?"

Fifty dollars was printed on the sheet.

Lucas answered first. "I eat anywhere that's free."

Marilyn smiled and handed it to him. "It's all yours. I won it in a raffle, but you know I don't care for eating out. Too noisy. I thought you two could enjoy it."

Trina's heart stalled. She sucked in a quiet breath, but a wicked grin spread across Lucas's face.

"Thanks." He turned to her. "How about tonight?"

"I…" Brayden was home with his grandmas. Knowing Mom and Sarah, there was nothing planned but work and the ten o'clock news. Brayden was either running around or painting the back deck. Or both because that was how the kid did chores. "I'll have to call Mom."

"Oh, I'm so glad that worked out. Tell me how the food is." She was about to go back to her office, but she looked at Lucas. "Did you remember Cassie's wedding this weekend?"

The hand holding the gift certificate dropped to his side. "No, I forgot."

Trina's mind spun through any Cassies she knew. Lucas had a cousin with that name.

Marilyn nodded as if it was perfectly understandable that he'd forgotten his cousin's wedding that was less than a week away. "I'll support you either way. Lord knows, you shouldn't have to go. But she called asking if you were bringing a plus one. I guess some guests cancelled and they wanted to verify their numbers. Save money."

"Because that's more important." The bitterness in Lucas's voice was surprising. He slid his assessing gaze toward Trina. Marilyn followed suit.

The roof could've opened and shone a spotlight right on her. That's what it felt like under the weight of their stares.

"What do you say?" Lucas asked. "Want to hang around a bunch of family that will simultaneously be nice to me and pretend I don't exist, all while planning to comment as soon as I leave on how bullheaded and cheap I am to not bring a gift?"

Well, when he said it like that, she wouldn't miss it. "We can approach this a couple of different ways. I can find an outfit that shows more than it covers and stagger around like I had a few too many."

Lucas's eyes twinkled and his shoulders relaxed. "Only if you mutter about an hourly rate."

"Or I can borrow Sarah's winter clothes. The ones that cover her from her chin to her toes because she's always cold, and I'll complete the look with tights and loafers. I'll find some glasses and ask everyone if they want to hear about my frog neurogenesis project and guess the most number of mutated limbs I've found on one toad." Who even knew if what she'd said was a thing, but it sounded fun.

Marilyn snorted. "Like I said, whatever you decide, I'll support. Just don't use that gift certificate for their gift. Treat yourself." She went back into her office, shaking with laughter.

"So…dinner?" Lucas's smile was sweeter, less mischievous.

"If I go to dinner with you, you owe me the story." Trina glanced down at her gunmetal-gray scrubs. "I have to run home and change first."

"I'll pick you up." The hot look he gave her before he swaggered back to his dad's room said they would be talking about more than his family drama.

Suddenly, she'd never looked forward to a meal more.

LUCAS FLEW DOWN the gravel road. His old truck rattled up the hill and crested. The dip in the landscape housed both his place and the Harts'. Thick rows of trees separated Trina's home from the stock pond and pasture. Then there was the thin row between their properties before he reached his house.

He turned down the Harts' driveway, excitement bubbling in his veins like it was a first date. He shouldn't be this happy about tonight. Trina didn't act as if she wanted him in the long term, but while his brain kept ordering him to quit pursuing her, he couldn't. That way lay heartbreak. Shaylee had thrown herself at him. But when the realities of farming and paying for Dad's care had hit, she'd blamed him —for everything—and had withdrawn.

And nothing had changed. His other pickup was done and ready to sell. It'd help pay for another two months for Dad. Covering the debt of the divorce and paying Shaylee her half had cleaned him out. He'd kept his operation afloat, managing not to hand over everything to the government. But he lived unstable paycheck to paycheck.

His best friend's dad had worked for him for a few months. Lucas had even applied for a few jobs in town, since Aaron's dad didn't ask for much in compensation. But then his wife's interior design business took off and he'd left to help her.

Business was better with her and Lucas couldn't blame him. His motto after the divorce had become *I don't have anything to offer.*

Parking in front of the house, he let the engine idle. Before he could climb out, Trina banged out the door. To anyone else, she wore simple jeans and a white tank top under an emerald button-up shirt. But he knew those jeans. The studded pockets made the sway of her hips mesmerizing.

The front door opened again. Brayden came out, a Minute Maid lemonade in his hand.

A pang hit his heart. He hadn't had a lemonade since before Dad's accident. After the dust had literally and figuratively settled, he'd tossed everything in that fridge. It was full of beer now.

But he should grab a pack of lemonade. Since Brayden was over more.

Trina got in and Lucas pulled away, waving at Brayden.

"What'd you tell him?" Lucas prepped himself for some excuse about how insignificant he was to her.

"That you got a gift card and didn't want to eat alone."

Okay. That wasn't so bad.

"I also said that I was going to your family's wedding this

weekend for moral support." She folded her arms across her chest and looked at him. "And then I ended up with Mom's opinion of that side of your family, and when Sarah came in, I think Brayden learned a few more colorful words."

Without those two, he wasn't sure he could've survived those first few years after Dad had relinquished the farm. Sarah and Davina planted and harvested their own silage and had watched cattle prices for decades. Being around their business had given him more insight into farming than he'd ever had before. Sarah had taught him how to follow the markets and Davina had passed on her knowledge of all things tractor and harvesting, including how to capitalize on the weather.

"Did Sarah tell you about the time she and Aaron's dad were out with me until midnight bringing the fields in?" He shook his head. The storm the weather service had predicted had hit worse than expected. He would've lost most of his crop.

"I believe that was mentioned after 'bleepity-bleep bastards left a kid in charge without lifting a finger. But if they had, they would've bleepity-bleep charged him for it.'"

Those times were too dark to laugh about, but he found himself doing it anyway. "My uncle Dwight, Dad's brother, said he could help, but when he started talking percentages, I asked him how the fuck I was supposed to give away half my profits and not go under. Then he wanted me to sell. To him, of course, but when I brought it up to Davina, she stormed into her office and brought out papers about how much my land was worth. Way more than Uncle Dwight had offered."

"That's despicable."

He shrugged. "That's my family. When Mom died, her side came after her life insurance. I guess that was the plus side of being married to Shaylee. No one was taking money she thought was hers."

"Holy shit, Lucas. That's awful. And Cassie is Uncle Dwight's girl?"

"Yep. And I've been informed that if I don't show, I'm making the day about me and not her."

"And I'll bet they didn't invite Herman."

His grip tightened on the steering wheel. No, they hadn't. It probably bothered Aunt Marilyn that one of her brothers wanted to forget the existence of the other. She didn't mention it and he didn't ask. He supported her. She supported him. Having Trina along would help make the night less an obligation and more a… Nope, still an obligation for people who'd never had his best interests at heart and who'd ghosted him when he'd needed support the most.

"To them, Dad died a long time ago." But he was still dying, a little bit at a time. "I think Uncle Dwight's convinced Dad doesn't need to be in a home. You know, a waste of money when I could care for him."

"That's so awful. He's not gone and neither are you." Trina sounded so understanding. He hadn't realized how few people he could talk to—about any of this. "I think your mom did pretty damn well. You still have the farm and your dad's getting really good care, like he should be."

Lucas's voice was rough when he spoke. "He, uh… Dad wouldn't have wanted to, you know, live this way. But… I can't just let him—" His throat thickened too much to speak.

"Lucas, pull over." He did as she said without question. When he was stopped a half mile from the maintenance shop at the edge of town, she twisted in her seat. "Let's get this straight right now. No one expected you to let your dad suffer. And the Herman I know wouldn't have wanted you to take care of all his bodily needs while trying to keep the farm he'd built going. He can't be on his own, and he needs to be with professionals who know how to care for him."

He nodded, his jaw flexing so hard he was afraid it'd lock up.

She faced forward again. "Fuck Uncle Dwight."

He barked a laugh. "You know how many times I've thought that?" He'd never said it out loud. Dad had idolized his brother, even during the times Mom had complained about how the man was only out for himself. "Fuck Uncle Dwight."

Kicking the pickup into gear, he drove the rest of the way with a stupid grin on his face.

CHAPTER 6

*T*rina took the paper ring that had encased her fork and knife in a napkin and folded it into an airplane. The ride here had given her too much insight into Lucas. The defensive wall she'd built against him was crumbling. No wonder he'd never talked to her. He was too busy fortifying his life against his shitty family.

Her own dad was a piece of work who'd left and not looked back. He justified his absence by claiming to be a victim of his ex-wife's identity. Better to be gone than to face any embarrassment that he hadn't been man enough.

Of course, Trina had informed him that a real man would support his kid. Her last words to him before he'd hung up. She didn't even know where he lived now.

At least Pax had stayed in Moore. Brayden adored his dad, but he was getting old enough to question Pax's behavior.

Why does he go see Emily's family when he planned time with me?

Why can't Dad and Emily move into a bigger condo? Then they wouldn't have to complain about how cramped it is when I stay over.

Lucas set his menu down. "Did you decide what you want?"

She'd picked her food based on cost. She wasn't pushing the bill over fifty. While he'd been deciding what to eat, she'd looked around. There were a lot of familiar faces. The bar side of the joint probably had more people she knew. In the far corner was a man with his wife and small child. His gaze passed over her. The flicker of recognition was followed by alarm. His tanned skin turned waxen.

Yep. She fully recalled the way he'd been hitting on one of the other bartenders. His advances had gotten so bad that Trina had stepped in with one last warning: *hands to yourself or we're calling the cops.*

There were so many reasons why she didn't date, and this was one of them. Before Brayden had been born, she'd picked up extra work at other bars to compensate for her lack of benefits. Alongside all the celebrations she'd witnessed over the years was the behavior that had made her question why she'd chosen the field of food service and entertainment in the first place. Infidelity, violence, addiction.

Sometimes she couldn't even get groceries without crossing paths with someone who'd been an unruly drunk the previous weekend.

"Trina?" Lucas ducked his head like he was trying to get into her line of vision. "You still with me?"

"Sorry. I don't get out much, and being here reminded me why." At his questioning look, she explained. "The dad in the corner was a guy I almost kicked out two weeks ago for hitting on Annie. Don't look, but there's a couple sitting by the door. They're swingers."

Lucas failed to keep from looking at the fiftyish couple

sharing an onion blossom. They looked like the upper middle-class white couple found in any picture frame sold in department stores across the country. "Seriously?"

"As a spilled beer. Which is fine, but they keep asking me about Sarah. Would they go up to anyone else and ask if their mom or dad wants to swing?" She took a sip of water but wasn't done. "And the big guy who just walked into the bar? Last month, he complained to my boss that I was watering down his drinks."

"Were you?"

She nodded. "Because that's what my boss, Freddie, told me to do. 'Add extra ice and take a buck off the price.' The guy has a mean streak when he's drunk, but he and Freddie are fishing buddies, and Freddie doesn't have the balls to ban him from the bar. So I get to deal with him."

Lucas's expression darkened. "That's not right."

She shrugged. "Better me than a sweetie like Annie."

"You don't think you're a sweetie?"

She shot him a scowl. His grin lit up their little corner of the dining area. She had to look away. The man had a dimple and she wanted to lick it every time it appeared.

The server saved her by coming to take their order. Alone again, the heat of Lucas's gaze washed over her. Conversation wasn't her strong suit. She could small talk someone, but usually her customers led the way and she'd just "really" and "you don't say" her way through.

"Anyone in here you have good memories of?" Lucas asked.

She blinked. "Why?"

He lifted a shoulder, his gaze touching on the three people she'd pointed out earlier. "Just curious."

She mulled over his question. The truth was, no, she didn't recognize one single person in here that struck a positive chord. Growing up in Moore and working at one of the most popular joints in town for nearly ten years meant she probably knew the lion's share of the people surrounding them.

Sure, they were familiar, but not enough to recall an interaction or even their regular drink.

No, wait. The couple that had just walked into the bar were around her moms' age. They weren't regulars, but they weren't strangers. Nice people, always asked how she was doing. Whiskey sour and a Bloody Mary, extra olives. But she didn't know their names. Jeff? Enid? Or Jess and Evan?

Lucas waited patiently for her answer. Why was it so hard to say something?

"I don't remember the good ones," she finally admitted. "I may know them as good tippers, or if they're regulars." Like John and Emma? No, that wasn't right either. "They leave me alone and I leave them alone."

And she wasn't a part of their life any more than that.

Lucas leaned forward, his elbows on the table. The space between them closed until she realized she was pressed against the back of the booth.

"I have a hard time believing you don't know more than what they order." He pointed to where the couple had disappeared. "Where does Joe work?"

Joe! And his wife, Eva. A basket of buns and small plates were set on the table and she reached for the plates to hand out. Lucas tapped her hand.

"You're not waiting on me tonight." He set a bun on her plate and slid it over.

The gesture was sweet, even if it was partially scolding. Doling out buns would've given her something to do besides watch him and remember how delicious being pinned to her couch under his body had been.

To distract herself, she mined her memories for more

information on the couple. She'd known them for years but didn't *know* them.

How often had she waited on Joe? He tipped well. And while he was one of the brawniest guys she'd ever seen, he was also the friendliest. He came in with durable jeans, like he did outdoor work, and he wore denim work shirts that had some emblem she never paid attention to. Joe kept his hair cut trim and tight, and his dark skin was a few shades lighter than his deep brown eyes. He had a laugh that boomed across the room and made others smile just for hearing it.

Looked like she'd paid more attention than she'd thought. Sometimes Joe came in with his wife, sometime she was with people Trina assumed were coworkers. At least once a year, she wove her black hair into braids that she tied in a bun. Summer. That was during the summer. But no matter the season, Eva dressed in business-casual wear, and when she arrived with others of the same slacks-and-heeled-shoes variety, it was around five thirty, and they cleared out by seven. Just like Joe, they were polite and tipped well but always split the bill separately.

"I don't know where Joe or Eva works," she finally admitted. "But I remember for one Halloween, Eva was in shorts and a basketball jersey. I heard her tell someone it was her old one."

"Eva's my insurance agent and Joe is the head of the county works department."

"You get a gold star for knowing my customers better than I do." She took a bite of her bun, but it might as well have been chalk dust. Her bitchiness was out of place. Along with getting a degree, maybe she needed to think about going out for fun again.

Hurt flickered in his gaze. "I don't know the swingers."

"I don't think Joe and Eva do either." His smile prompted

her to continue. "Look, most people who come in want to socialize, but not with the staff. Many are nice enough, but we're there to serve. They pay us. Don't think for one minute that if I have a bad night and fuck up, a disgruntled customer won't demand to speak to my boss, even if they just smiled and said thanks two minutes earlier."

"Point taken." His bun was untouched. Had she ruined his appetite?

"And before you point out that it'll be the same when I'm a nurse, I know."

"That's a perk of being self-employed. One of the only ones," he muttered.

Something in his tone caught. He sounded resigned. "Are you thinking of quitting farming?"

His chuckle was bitter. "I've been thinking of getting out since the ink dried. I think I might have to get a part-time job or something."

"Why? You just told me you fought to save that place from your greedy relatives."

"No, I saved it from getting sold dirt cheap."

A whole world of difference in the wording. "Do you want to sell?"

"Want to? No. But if I can't find something to help pay for Dad's care, then…" He shoved the bun in his mouth whole, like a plug to keep himself from saying more.

Those times he'd glowered into his beer, or had a few too many. She'd assumed it was divorce fallout, or that he was making her life harder just for the attention. All that time, he'd been worried about his dad's care.

"What would you do?" She waited for him to finish chewing. He wasn't getting off the hook. He'd made her think too deeply about why she only hung on to the bad memories of bartending, so he could open a vein himself.

He snorted as he swallowed and wiped his mouth. "What

can I do? Most farmers today have gone to college. I had to come home and take over before I finished my degree. All I have is on-the-job training and no other education."

And he couldn't afford to go to school *and* pay for a roof over his dad's head. "You have a lot of skills."

"As much as I'd love to go out and apply, I can't really sit through an interview and say 'the business I run all by myself is failing, no I didn't finish college, and my wife walked out on me because I couldn't provide enough for her, but hey, you should hire me.'" He spotted the server heading their way with plates of steaming food and finished in a rush. "It's up to me to figure out how the hell I can keep going on what I have."

He rewarded the server with a friendly smile and dug into his food like there was nothing more to talk about.

WHAT THE HELL had he been thinking, capitalizing on Aunt Marilyn's spur-of-the-moment gift card and then confessing all his insecurities before the main course was even served?

No wonder he never had to sit and ponder why Shaylee had left him.

He and Trina were friends, and it wasn't like he had a bunch of them to go to. Aaron had his own family to worry about and didn't need to waste mental time on him. He'd gotten to know Aaron's cousin Justin and Justin's best friend Caleb really well, but they'd settled down too. No way was he crying on any of their shoulders.

He'd put up with too many pitying looks from Shaylee's friends.

There's the poor farmer she saddled herself with.

He sawed into his prime rib. This was the best he was going to eat for a while. Except for next weekend at the wedding, where he planned to inhale his full share of the bridal buffet without bringing a gift. Petty? Hell, yes.

He eyed Trina as she concentrated on her baked potato. Sour cream, chives, and a little cheese. She'd ordered chicken and he knew damn well it wasn't because she preferred her own ranch's beef. The gift card was for fifty dollars and Trina was making sure they stayed under it, and that was before he'd confessed how hard up he was for cash.

There was no point arguing. She would've probably stuck with a side salad out of spite. At least her Monterey chicken looked good.

The meal passed in near silence. Every so often, Lucas caught the guy she'd pointed out earlier stealing glimpses of her. The one she'd been ordered to cut off and taken the brunt of the consequences for.

Her boss was a coward.

She'd make a good nurse. Compassionate without letting it affect her work. Her patients and their families would look up to her. Then she'd be out of his orbit, making decent money and helping others.

People argued that he provided food for the nation. But when his hard work for the past year sat in piles on the ground at the elevator, he didn't feel like a productive member of society.

Couple that with the decreasing market prices, and most days he dragged himself to bed as drained as corn prices.

Noise from the bar rose as a band kicked off. Bass pounded the walls and all chance of a nice visit without shouting fled. But they hadn't been doing much talking. Her presence saved him from going next door and begging Joe for a job. He'd done that once, but Joe only had one part-time job with benefits in the county shop, and the only thing that'd make a person leave a position like that was death or retirement.

The guy working it now might be close to retiring, hopefully not dying, but any other applicant would have official training, probably even a degree of some kind. He had a whole lot of nothing.

Trina smiled at the server as she declined a water refill. The bill was left on the table. He grabbed it.

"Ready to go?" he asked. He'd coerced her into dinner out and attending the wedding with him. She didn't need to waste her Friday night staring across the table at him.

Looking at her and the way her gaze darted around as she read the room was entertaining as hell. She couldn't shut if off. The lights glinted off her short hair, highlighting some strands with a honey hue. Pixie. That was how he'd describe her now. But one that could cut you.

"I'll meet you outside. I've gotta visit the restroom." She slid out of the booth and he paid, only needing to leave a little extra to cover the tip.

The space between his shoulder blades tightened. He hated to miss walking out with her, but Trina wasn't the type that expected to be doted on. Didn't mean she didn't deserve it.

Standing inside by the door seemed too clingy, so he stepped out and waited off to the side, nodding at another young couple heading in.

The sun was dipping lower in the sky, and the building blocked the horizon. Trina banged out the door and went straight for the pickup without noticing him. Lucas was about to call for her when the man who'd given her problems exited after.

"Hey, Trina," the guy growled. He listed to the side, but caught himself. Drunk.

Trina stiffened, but she kept going.

"You don't have anything to say tonight? I find that hard

to believe," he slurred. His volume kicked up. "Get back here and talk to me."

Lucas treaded carefully behind him. "The lady isn't interested in talking to you."

The man spun around, stumbling to keep from falling. Trina had heard him and stopped, her eyes full of anxiety. How close had this customer of hers gotten to violence?

Lucas held his arms up like he was surrendering, though he had no intention to. None of them needed a fight in the parking lot. "Look man, do you have a ride home?"

The other guy sneered. "I don't need a ride home. Butt *the fuck* out. This is between me and her."

"I'm her date, so it's kind of involving me." Lucas circled around the drunk to block him from Trina.

"Date?" The chortle was mixed with a healthy dose of phlegm. "She don't do men."

She "don't do men," or she "don't do" *this* man? Is that where his bitterness was stemming from?

"I'm not working tonight, Anthony," Trina said. "What you do isn't my business."

Lucas was a few yards away from her, but not close enough. The three of them were in a triangular formation and he wanted to block her from this nastiness.

She tipped her head toward the building, calm, controlled, the pink hues of the sunset reflecting in her hazel eyes. "Why don't you go back inside?"

"And do what?" Anthony's face turned a blotchy red. "They cut me off!"

Trina shook her head. "Not because of me."

Anthony squinted at her like he didn't believe it. "Wanna bet? I don't think it's a coincidence that you're here and I quit getting served." He lurched forward, but Lucas cut in front of him. It was getting harder to avoid an altercation.

There was no pride in beating down a drunk guy, but the

force it'd take to stop someone who *maybe* wouldn't know better on a good day could affect his own ability to work.

The roar of the bar echoed into the night as the door opened. A familiar couple came out.

Joe held the door for his wife. Lucas kept from rolling his eyes skyward. He couldn't take his gaze off Anthony. But to Joe, it'd look like he was involved in a bar fight. Goodbye chances of ever getting hired. *Thanks a fucking lot, Anthony.*

"What's going on here?" Joe jerked his chin over his shoulder. Eva nodded and headed in the opposite direction. If only he could send Trina with her, but Anthony's bleary focus was still on her.

Anthony's head snapped around and he instantly relaxed, swaying to the side as he did. "Nothing, sir."

Joe's keen gaze assessed the situation, his gaze settling on Trina.

Her stance didn't scream everything was okay. Her feet were set wide, her hands balled at her side. "We were just suggesting that Anthony find a ride home."

"Uh-huh." Joe's dark eyes jumped from her to Anthony. The gray streaking through Joe's black hair didn't detract from the power he emanated. "How 'bout I call you a cab, Tony? It's on me."

"No—" Anthony cleared his throat. "That'd be fine, thanks." His gaze stuck on the ground.

Joe waved them off, his phone already in his hand. "You two go ahead. Tony here is one of my employees. I'll make sure he gets home, but I sure do appreciate you two looking after him."

"Thanks, Joe." Trina's voice was softer than Lucas had ever heard it.

The threat tonight was over. But what would happen the next time Trina came across Anthony when he'd been drinking?

She didn't speak as she got into his pickup. Why'd he parked so far back in the parking lot? Next time he'd find a spot under a streetlamp. It wasn't dark enough for them to be on, but that didn't matter when it came to Trina's safety.

He hit the door lock as if Anthony were going to appear out of thin air and grab her. The keys were sliding into the ignition when she slammed the armrest up and slid over. He was about to ask what was wrong when her lips were on his and she dissolved into him.

He hugged her to him and wished the seats were pushed all the way back so they could recline together. But something about this scenario didn't feel right and it didn't have to do with being in the middle of a parking lot.

Pulling away, he caught her heavy-lidded gaze. "Are you okay?"

She bit her lip and tried to put distance between them.

He tightened his hold and gave her a flat look. "Talk to me."

"Adrenaline, I guess." Her mouth was puffy and he couldn't quit looking at it.

"Do you have to deal with that shit all the time?"

She nodded. "It's usually in the bar, where I have some backup. When he first yelled at me…" A shudder ran through her and he rubbed her back until her tension drained. "I thought I was trapped out there all alone. And then you were there."

He wanted to say that he'd always be there, but that was a lie. She'd move on, but she should always have someone watch her back.

A ghostly laugh wafted across her face. "I'm not usually the damsel gushing over her dude savior."

A smile lifted the corner of his mouth. "I'm not usually a dude savior. And as much as I like this, if we're going to do something together, it won't be like this." He had enough hang-ups when it came to sex; wondering if she felt beholden to him wasn't going to be one of them.

"Right." She scooted back into her seat and pushed a hand through her short hair. "You're right." A sigh escaped her and she stared out the window.

She was getting stuck in her head. He could see it. She was critiquing her reaction to Anthony, how she'd acted out of her norm with him just now, and he couldn't let that happen. "Hold on." He dug out his phone. "I'm going to turn my camera to record. Can you say that again?"

A cute little line formed in her brow. "Say what?"

"'You're right, Lucas.' "

She shot him a glare and playfully swatted him. He couldn't quit laughing as he started the engine and pulled away. This was his comfort zone. He knew what to do with a woman who was irritated at him.

CHAPTER 7

"You aren't going to the actual wedding?" Mom leaned against Trina's bedroom door, her sinewy arms crossed over her chest. Mom was shorter than her by two inches, but packed more muscle than she could ever hope to. The beer cases she hefted at work didn't match the bulk of a hay bale.

"No, just the reception. Lucas's compromise." She had told Mom the real reason she was going to the wedding. Not the fake dating part. Mom was pretty casual about life, but she had a soft spot for Lucas that was a county wide.

"It's nice seeing you two talk again."

She wasn't the one who had offed communication in the first place. "He can be a decent guy."

"He's more than decent." Mom let out a disgusted noise. "He was definitely more decent than Shaylee deserved."

And wasn't that the kicker. *Shaylee* had left *him*. Lucas wasn't the type to have a quick fuck and walk away. Or several quick fucks. He'd want more. Would he want more after a free supper and a contentious wedding reception? He hadn't said anything. She didn't expect proclamations of undying love, but after her dating life, she knew the signs of a commitment-phobe. No promises. Casual attitude. Good times all around.

She was usually the one to display them.

Finding someone to grow old with wasn't a priority. Taking care of herself and Brayden was. She'd actively discouraged relationships after the fallout with Pax and the fear he'd left her with that she could've been entwined with someone like that for the rest of her life.

"He's free of her now." And before his life had gotten permanently tangled with hers. If Lucas and Shaylee had had a kid, Shaylee would've possessed all the power. Lucas didn't seem like the type to handle that sort of arrangement well. It'd kill him to be cut out of his kid's life. Especially if Shaylee objected to visits with Herman. Or maybe that was her own intense dislike of Shaylee coloring her assumptions.

Lucas would be hurt enough if his ex-wife was indeed expecting by the man she'd left him for.

And that was the real reason Trina was going to the stupid wedding. So when Shaylee paraded around in maternity outfits, threw baby showers at his church, and sent announcement cards to what was left of their circle of friends, he wouldn't have the shitty memory of this wedding heaped onto him too.

"Yeah, he's free." Mom's tone was loaded, but she knew better than to push it. She was testing the waters. She'd used the same not-quite hints when Trina was rundown and enduring morning sickness. *When you're ready to tell me why you can't keep crackers down, I'm right here.* "You look good."

"I'm wondering if I should wear my Miss Me jeans and a nice shirt instead." She studied her yellow sundress. Her arms were tanned from the work she'd been doing on the ranch to help pay for room and board. She'd even styled her short hair. It was wicked over to one side in a little peak.

Sassy. Fitting, or so she'd heard. The shoes were just strappy sandals. This was the first time she'd ever worn them—because she'd bought them yesterday. Not because she was looking forward to the wedding. Her justification was that they were essential, like armor. The more presentable she looked, the less they could fault Lucas for attending.

"If I said no, would that make a difference?" Mom squinted. "Holy *shi*-it. Are you wearing lipstick?"

Trina sucked her lips in, wanting to deny it. "Tinted lip gloss. We need to put on a show." There was also the fake-dating ruse to keep up. Marilyn's grudge against Mom and Sarah wasn't going to keep her out of nursing school.

"Uh-huh." Mom rolled off the doorframe, threw her a *sure you are* look, and wandered away. "Speak of the devil, Lucas is pulling up."

Trina flew downstairs to give Brayden a kiss on the head.

"Is Lucas here?" Brayden was already pushing off the floor.

"Yeah, but we gotta go, kiddo. He's not coming in to visit." That'd be too close to a real date, too much of a meet-the-parents scenario. And since her moms loved him, they'd risk being late for the reception.

Brayden bounced on his toes. "Can I just say hi?"

Damn Lucas and the way he'd wormed himself into her son's heart. Any male showing interest in him after his lackadaisical father's treatment might as well wear a cape. Her son wanted to play with Lucas every chance he got.

Boots hit the porch deck, underscoring the voices filtering through the door. Sarah must be chatting with Lucas. She was worse than Brayden.

Deep male laughter stirred the excitement in her belly. Twice now, she'd had her lips on his and it wasn't enough.

She'd have to be careful around him. And keep her distance.

She whipped open the door, Brayden hot on her heels. He rushed around her and tackled Lucas.

A grunt came from Lucas, but he grinned. His eyes were glued to her, sweeping from her hair to her metallic-purple-polished toenails and back up, lingering on her lips. Damn him, he knew she'd put on makeup too.

It was everything she could do to keep her gaze on his face. There was no way she'd let her own gaze dip down and see how well his crisp black jeans hugged his strong thighs. She knew without checking that he was wearing his polished black cowboy boots. The Stetson on his head—also black—shaded his eyes, making them darker and hot enough to burn her dress off.

He swept the hat off his head and held it over the wrinkle-free white button-up shirt with green pinstripes. The lopsided grin was her first warning that he was going to say something to embarrass her.

"Excuse me, ma'am. I'm here for Trina Hart. She usually wears worn jeans and a T-shirt. She's always scowling—" He narrowed his eyes and leaned closer, his other hand coming around Brayden's shoulders. "Oh, there you are."

Her scowl was in full effect. The effort it took not to laugh was stronger than expected. But wasn't that what always happened around Lucas? "Brayden wanted to say hi."

Mom stepped out from behind her, exchanging knowing looks with Sarah. Trina couldn't shoot her a warning glare without tipping off Lucas. Mom's brow arched, screaming her incredulity that tonight was only about moral support. "You two have fun. Brayden, come out to the garden when you're done."

Brayden let Lucas go. "When are you coming over again?"

Lucas looked at her, his eyes full of question—and a healthy dose of mirth.

Trina let the door slam behind her before the house filled

with mosquitos. "I'll talk to him tonight, but don't get your hopes up. Lucas is a busy guy."

Lucas's smile faded. "I'll always make time."

Trina brushed her lips across Brayden's hair. "Go help Gramma." When he ran off, she asked Lucas, "Ready?"

"You look good," he said.

"Thanks. You too." The perfunctory compliment didn't give away just how good she thought he looked. "So the wedding is going on now, and by the time we get to Normandy, we'll hit the reception?"

"That's the plan. Aunt Marilyn is at the wedding now, but she'll sit with us at the reception." They both climbed into his freshly washed pickup. Trina eyed the inside. Also newly vacuumed and dusted. This wedding was a big deal.

Inspecting his pickup helped her not think about how they'd have to act around Marilyn. "What's Marilyn have against Mom and Sarah?"

"Nothing." Lucas's expression was perplexed. "Didn't they go to school together?"

"Sarah moved here after college. Mom and Marilyn maybe. I guess they're the same age." Trina stared out the window at the passing scenery. Lucas was taking the back roads to the highway, and the route was more scenic. More farms than ranches dotted the landscape. Like Mom always said, not all land was good for farming. Lucas's spread was perfect. Flat prairie land that was neatly sectioned out. Her family's spot was situated between Lucas's property and another large farm. Spring-fed ponds and natural copses of trees broke up the space. Perfect for cattle, not for tractors.

"Maybe Davina got the guy?"

Trina would've expected more humor in Lucas's words, but he was serious. It made sense. A grudge over a guy. Her dad? "Then Marilyn should thank Mom for saving her the heartache of living with him."

"Yeah. I don't think she knows about any of that."

Surprise drifted through her and right back out. Their town was small; why wouldn't Marilyn know? Nathan Hart hadn't saved his derision for private. But Trina was just Lucas's neighbor. Why would Lucas or his family care about her family's troubles? Now that Dad had been gone for more than twenty years, everyone forgot.

Well, this convo was depressing. "How are the fields doing?"

The rest of the way to Normandy, they talked about his farm, what crops he planted—as if she couldn't look out the window and see, but she asked anyway. He explained his reasoning behind what he planted where, how he treated his fields, and what his harvest plan was. Then he peppered her with questions about the ranch. She answered but thought about how well-informed he was about his own industry. Did he even realize how enthused he sounded about market prices, commodities, and farm equipment?

Or had Shaylee done her best to stomp the love for his career into the hard-packed ground?

When they spotted buildings on the edge of town, they both quieted.

Time to play the game.

Lucas weaved through the few side streets. They didn't need an address. Normandy was small enough. Find the building with all the cars around it. A small, mason-block community center that had probably been a church at one time was close to the center of town. Cars and pickups, heavy on the pickups, lined the streets circling the building.

He parked a block and a half away. The walk would help work off some of her nerves. She came around the front of the pickup. He waited for her and held out his hand.

She looked at it like it was a cobra in disguise. Making out could be written off as hormones. She hadn't been with anyone since she'd moved home. Before that…her prospects had been limited, and getting herself off was less complicated. But holding hands? That was so…intimate. The action carried a lot more meaning than any hookup she'd ever had.

"For show, right?" he said.

Oh. For show. The feeling of being let down was all too familiar. She stuffed her hand in his and stared straight ahead. His grip was warm around hers and could easily be an anchor for her heart, but she wasn't going to allow it. Keeping her clasp loose, she strutted toward the community center, calling on all the confidence and attitude people thought she had. Little did they know that most of the time, she rose to meet their expectations. It got exhausting.

When they reached the building, he held open the plate-glass door. Music and laughter ballooned in volume the closer they got to the dance-floor entrance. A young girl waited at a table outside the door with a large guest book open in front of her.

Lucas leaned down to write their names. "Are you from the bride or groom's side?"

The girl swept her long hair off her silky cream dress. "I'm the bride's niece."

Lucas did a double take. "You're little Dori?"

"Yep." Dori went back to her phone, unimpressed that Lucas knew exactly who she was. "You can put your card and gift in the basket." She glanced up from her screen, her gaze going from Trina's empty hands to Lucas's, then back to her phone.

Lucas gave Trina a *God this sucks* look and grabbed her hand again. This time he held it like a lifeline. Or was that her? If Dori was anything like the reception they'd get inside, she wanted to abort the mission. Was it even worth it?

There was a lull in the music and someone started speaking through a microphone.

"Sounds like a toast," Lucas mumbled. "Should we wait?"

"Nope." Trina yanked the metal gym door open. Half the guests turned to see who was entering. The other half was riveted on what a guy her age in a tux was saying to the bride. The groom gushed about her in front of everyone. Trina should be ready to gag, but damn. How sweet was that? In front of everyone.

Whatever. Not like it lessened the chances of either one of them walking out at the first sign of trouble.

Lucas's keen gaze swept through the room. He spotted Marilyn first, seated at the far right corner of the room.

As the groom wrapped up the story of how they'd met and when he'd known Cassie was the one, she and Lucas snagged a glass of punch and small plates of hors d'oeuvres. She was starving and this was not going to be enough to eat.

They were almost to Marilyn's table when a woman approached. Her flame-red hair was the same color as the highlights that the sun had made in Lucas's hair when they were kids. The rays had bleached his hair, turning the reddish brown to fiery red. Was he ever outside without a hat long enough to get the same effect as an adult?

"Lucas! You made it." She gave him a quick hug. Lucas's smile was tight and even. Fake.

"Kelly. How've you been?"

"Oh, you know. Same old." Kelly turned toward her. The glaze in her eyes made Trina wonder how many drinks she'd had. Early celebrating? "Shaylee, you cut your hair. It's cute."

Cold mortification slicked down her spine. Her insides matched Lucas's frozen expression. Trina wasn't incensed over the mistake, she was pissed because it showed just how far removed from Lucas's life these people were. He'd gone through a divorce by himself.

"It's Trina."

Kelly blinked and shook her head. Did she really not understand that Trina wasn't Shaylee?

"She had an affair with the dentist she worked for, so it's easy to tell us apart. She'll have whiter teeth." Had she gone too far?

Lucas tried to cover a "holy shit" with a cough. "Shaylee and I have been divorced for a couple of years."

"Really?" The whisper-yell was incredulous. Had she really not heard at all? "I'm so sorry." She flashed Trina a smile that said she really didn't care. "Welcome, Trina. How long have you two been seeing each other?"

"A couple of months," Lucas said at the same time Trina uttered, "A few weeks."

Kelly's smile wavered. "O-Okay. Well, you two have fun." She clicked off in her four-inch heels.

Lucas stared after her. "Sorry."

"It's not your fault. Do they really not know you're divorced?"

"I guess they never heard it from me. I'm sure Aunt Marilyn mentioned something, but…"

"Yeah." Lucas's family hadn't thought it was important enough to remember.

Finally reaching Marilyn's table, she set her plate and drink down. Lucas did the same but pulled the chair out for her too. She stared at him.

"What? I'm a gentleman."

She wanted to say, "Since when?" but—Marilyn. "Thank you."

As they settled, Lucas asked how the wedding was. Marilyn gushed about the service and how nice everyone looked. But once that was done, she pinned them both with a pleasant stare. "So, what do you two have planned for the rest of the weekend?"

Now for the real stress of the night: lying to her boss.

~

THAT DAMN SUNDRESS kept sliding off Trina's knees and he had the hardest time not running his fingers along her satiny skin.

When she'd answered the door wearing a dress, she'd slayed him. Words had fled. She wore jeans. Always. Even as a kid, because they'd go running through fields and pastures. Her legs were as muscular and curvy as the rest of her. But her son and moms nearby had been enough to keep him from babbling about how sexy she was. She'd dressed up for him. That had to mean something.

Unless it was part of the act.

How long have you two been seeing each other?

He'd been seeing Trina for a long time. The real question was had she started paying attention?

The DJ fired up the music again, an upbeat country song played at a level that made it hard to converse.

Marilyn waved at the dance floor. "Don't let me stop you two."

Trina paused midsip of her punch. She still had a few chips on her plate.

"Take your time and finish eating." He tried not to yell in her ear. "Want a drink?"

"Absolutely."

He leaned close to speak into her ear without Marilyn hearing. "I'm probably supposed to know what you drink."

Goose bumps sprang up over her arms, and he took his time leaning away. She turned her head into him as he was pulling away. He tipped his face down, their proximity reminding him of being in the pickup with her the other night. "I'll have what you're having."

"I'm driving, honey. Just a soda for me."

Her eyes lightened with surprise and could he blame her?

The times he hadn't gotten trashed in the bar, he'd still drunk no less than three beers. An amount he hoped would wear off by the time he had to drive home in the wee hours of the night. No, he hadn't quit drinking, but he'd gotten smarter about it. Working in the morning while hungover only ended in disaster.

She scanned the crowd. Silver Coors Light cans littered the tables. The drink of choice for the Peterson clan. "Bud Light."

He was grinning as he asked Aunt Marilyn what she wanted. He hated leaving these two alone, but mostly he hated leaving himself alone to roam in the wilds of his family.

Making it to the cash bar without a run-in, he grabbed the two beers and a Diet Coke. When he turned, Cassie was waiting for him.

"I heard you were here, Lucas." Her face was flushed from dancing and the general new-bride radiance. Images of Shaylee on their wedding day filtered through his mind. When her garter had been auctioned off, she'd thrown saucy looks at the crowd to up the bid, her leg curved up on a chair. She'd danced with her bridesmaids, jumping and flailing her arms everywhere, while he'd drunk with his groomsmen. During the limo ride from the church to the dancehall, she'd stood in the open sunroof, whooping through town.

The day had been about her, not about them. And he'd been clueless.

She'll have whiter teeth. He was going to chuckle about that for days. Trina and Shaylee were nothing alike.

"Congratulations on your big day," he said.

Cassie smiled and looked around. "Aunt Marilyn said you were bringing a date. Anyone I know?"

"You remember Trina Hart from next door? You used to play with her when we were kids and you guys came over."

"Trina? I didn't know you guys were dating."

They weren't. This farce had started out as fun, but as soon as they'd both answered separately, it sucked. He wanted it to be real, but Trina had only agreed to play along. She was clear that they weren't a thing outside of her getting into nursing school. "It's new."

"I heard Shaylee's getting married." Cassie seemed to know all about his life. Was Kelly being obtuse, or just mean? "Seems kind of sudden but I guess they've been together for a few years."

A few years? The math was instant in his head. He'd been divorced two years. The papers hadn't taken long to go through. A clean split and she hadn't wanted a part of his house or the land. Just her share of the worth. Were relatives circling like vultures above his head, waiting for the perfect moment to pounce?

"Have they been engaged for long?" she asked, nudging him out of his ponderings.

So that was the reason he'd been invited. To get the lowdown on his sordid life. "You'll have to ask her. We don't really talk."

"Oh. I talked to her a few months ago." Cassie had the grace to look ashamed. "I invited her. But she didn't mention being engaged. That's why I was wondering."

Shock and hurt weren't a good mix but not an uncommon feeling around his family. "Oh." What else could he say?

What would Trina say?

Cassie's husband came up behind her, snaking his arms around her waist. Her smile was instant and she tilted her face up at him.

The groom tore his adoring gaze away from the bride. "Hey, Luke."

He held in his sigh. Nothing against the name Luke, but

he'd been Lucas since the day he was born. Everyone called him Lucas and anyone who didn't wasn't paying attention. "Congrats, man."

"You weren't at the church, were you?" Cassie asked.

He shook his head, but they both watched him like they expected an explanation. "I couldn't make it." That was all they'd get.

Cassie opened her mouth, then shut it again. She glanced to her left where her dad—his uncle—was ignoring his existence. "How's your dad doing?"

She sounded sincere. Could she really be genuine? "As good as he can be, considering." Deteriorating more each year.

The song was over and she inched closer, leaving the protective circle of her new husband's arms. She lowered her voice so only he heard. "I remember how he'd build you snow mountains from all the snow he cleared from the drive. I used to beg Mom and Dad to go to your house every winter."

"Well, I can build the same snow mounds for us to climb, but I don't know if it'll be the same fun as adults."

She giggled. "Add beer. It makes everything more fun."

He smiled, the first real one around his kin in a long time.

Cassie's smile faded. "Look, I'm sorry…about inviting…"

"S'okay. It all worked out."

"Yeah." She looked over her shoulder toward Trina chatting with Marilyn. His gaze stuck on her crossed legs and how much her dress had ridden up. Nothing unusual on anyone else, but Trina hid more than her feelings from people. Correction: she didn't hide her body, but she didn't reveal it, like she didn't reveal her true thoughts. "I think it did."

Cassie gave his arm a squeeze. A bridesmaid flagged her down and she was off, the groom not far behind.

Please, let that be the last family interaction of the night.

He went to the table, set the drinks down, and held out his hand as a slow beat started. "Wanna dance?"

He knew she didn't, but she must've read the look on his face. "Sure."

Aunt Marilyn reclined in her chair and took a drink of her beer, her expression satisfied that he and Trina seemed to be having a good time.

He didn't know what kind of time he was having, but he needed to hold Trina in his arms.

On the dance floor, she slipped her hand into his and wrapped her other arm around his shoulder. "What's wrong? I saw you talking to Cassie."

He ran through the conversation for her as he relaxed into the music. Trina was in his arms, causing tension in a different way, one he'd welcome anytime.

"I can't believe she did that." Trina shook her head.

He guided her past another couple, hugging her close, loving how her hips swayed under his hand. When they were back in a clear area on the dance floor, she didn't move away.

He murmured in her ear, "Cassie asked about Dad. I don't know what to think about that."

"Maybe she's one generation removed from her dick of a father, so she's half as horrible?"

"Part asshole. That makes a lot of sense, actually."

He dipped his head and continued to hold her close. The song was almost done and he didn't want to waste the rest of it.

As it came to an end, he murmured, "I know a secret."

"Hmm?"

"You can dance."

She pursed her lips to keep from smiling. "You breathe a word of it and I'll find you."

He laughed loud enough that it drew attention even

though a fast-paced song was starting. He twirled her back into his arms and hit a two-step. She effortlessly followed his lead.

They stayed on the dance floor the rest of the night. Hours of touching her, feeling her body glide under his, made him only want to end this night one way.

Did she want the same thing?

*A*ll she could think about was getting laid.

The pickup's headlights showered their glow over their surroundings, and the countryside flew by. It was after midnight. They'd snuck out as the bride and groom were announcing their own exit.

Trina squirmed. Her body was hot and heavy. The slide of her dress over her flushed skin only made her discomfort worse. Unlike all the other times in her life when she wanted to have sex, these desires were specific. Only one man would do and he wore a sexy grin, fitted jeans that showed off that fine ass of his, and disheveled hair under a cowboy hat. Why had he even brought it? He only wore it outside, and he could've gone the whole night without it. It was like he knew how crazy the whole getup drove her and did it on purpose.

But that was the thing about Lucas. It was the things he did when he wasn't aware of it that really got to her. Like offering to buy her cold beer because hers got warm while they were dancing. How he opened doors and put his hand on the small of her back to guide her through.

Normally, a move like that would make her defensive as

hell. She hated feeling like the little lady. Instead, she felt protected. Valued. Like he had to make sure she was okay and couldn't help himself.

Then there was the kicked-puppy expression he'd worn when he'd come back from getting them drinks the first time. The talk with Cassie had fucked with his head. The woman had invited his ex and then talked to him like she'd given a shit. Lucas got under her skin, but he wasn't prickly to anyone else.

With her, he was more forceful, less aware of his impact on her. She didn't know how to feel about it, and she was too jaded to hope that it meant she was special. If anything, she worried it meant that he saw her as nothing more than Trina, his next-door neighbor he wanted to fuck.

If last weekend hadn't shown her how badly he wanted her, tonight would've. The way he'd held her, how he'd never let go but kept her tucked in close to him until they'd moved as one unit.

The secret he thought he had was a lie. She couldn't really dance. Yes, she knew two steps forward, one step back—she wouldn't touch a line dance to save her soul—but Lucas made it easy. Following his lead was irritatingly easy.

He turned off the highway. Ten minutes and they'd be home. How could she go tuck herself into bed—alone?

"I don't want to wake everyone," she said, her voice rough. "I can walk home from your place."

He looked at her, the lights of the dash deepening the shadows of his face. "Okay" was all he said.

Just do what you normally do. Which was coarse flirtation with a neon sign over her head that read *Sex Only*. And she wouldn't even have to kick the guy out when they were done. She could leave and be home in a minute.

No words left her mouth. Tension clogged the cab. Was it all from her side?

He pulled into his yard and parked by the small back door. She concentrated on his home instead of how little she wanted to end the night. His house was in worse shape than hers, but if he was trying to do everything himself around here, it was like a game of Whac-A-Mole with all the projects that needed to be done.

When she slid out into the night air, she ordered her feet to walk in the direction of her own place. They knew the way without thinking. But she couldn't.

Lucas rounded the front of the pickup. He came to a stop right in front of her. "I can walk you home."

Her eyelids drifted shut at the deep rumble of his quiet offer. She opened her eyes. "Lucas, I don't want to go home yet."

His swallow was audible. "Do you want to come inside?"

She nodded, too cowardly to meet his gaze. Unfortunately, that meant her gaze was plastered all over his wide chest, just like she hoped to be soon.

He took her hand and led her to the door. He fumbled with his keys, swore, and finally got the door open.

They didn't stop at the entry, going straight for his bedroom. Yet he stopped outside of it and took his hat off to brush a hand through his hair. Was he afraid to invite her in?

She hadn't been in his house since she was a kid. Only the belongings had changed. In the dark, she made out bare spots on the walls where pictures of Shaylee and her family must've hung. The decorations still up weren't Lucas's taste. Too contemporary. Too neutral toned. He was an outdoorsy guy, and the soft hues of a cottage were not his style.

She grabbed his hand and tugged him through the doorway.

She stepped out of her sandals and like he was following her lead, he toed out of his boots. She was about to whip off her dress, because *let's do this*, but he stopped her by trailing a finger over her collarbone.

"I think you look good all the time, but when I get to see your bare legs like this…" He took one last lingering look before bunching the hem of her dress in his hands. As more of her skin was bared, he groaned. "Your body is amazing."

They weren't naked—they hadn't even kissed yet tonight—but he made her feel sexier than any other date in her life. "I'd like to see yours."

Air whispered over her skin as he drew the dress over her head. "My farmer's tan is going to make you wet."

A laugh escaped her. "You keep surprising me with how good your butt looks in your jeans, so I can't wait to see it."

His gaze ran over the nicest bra she owned, which meant no frayed edges, down to her beige underwear. Then it shot up to her face as her words sank in. "My butt?"

"No, the other guy I'm pretending to be in a relationship with." Would the joke splash cold water on the night?

"*That* guy? He doesn't rock a beer gut like me."

"You can't have a beer belly if you don't drink much beer."

He feathered his hands along her chest, not dipping into her bra, only teasing. "I came too close to making a stupid mistake that could get me injured or killed. And since I don't have only myself to worry about, I had to stop with the self-pity."

She cupped his face. All those times in the bar, she'd been disgusted with him, but he'd been hurting and had no one to turn to. He'd taken care of himself and kept going like he always did. "Lucas—"

"Enough about the past. Just you and me right now." He captured her mouth, and the words she'd wanted to say vanished. Her body lit up like a live wire and everywhere he touched was a zap of power.

She opened for him immediately, licking her tongue along his. But the contact wasn't enough.

She continued the kiss but worked on unbuttoning his shirt. She yanked it down his shoulders, her torso brushing against his. Skin on skin. Heat licked over her body. Before the shirt hit the floor, she was tugging his jeans down.

Breaking the kiss, she stepped back to get a good look at him. She didn't want to think about previous partners here with Lucas, but another difference stood out. She'd never cared. She'd been attracted enough to be willing to sleep with others and that had been it.

But what did Lucas look like in all his glory?

Broad shoulders, thick biceps, and a muscled chest. He wasn't sporting a six- or an eight-pack, but that didn't diminish his effect. He looked good. Fit. A tapered waist and powerful thighs almost stole her attention, but it was the erection she wanted to touch.

She circled her fingers around him. He tipped his head back and groaned. Thick and searing hot, he twitched in her hand.

"Keep doing that and I'm going to embarrass myself." He claimed her mouth again and wrestled with her bra clasp. Fumbled and tried again.

She'd think he'd never done it before but obviously he wasn't a virgin. Reaching behind her, she released the hooks. The bra hit the floor.

This time he ended the kiss to stare at her. She hooked her fingers under the waistband of her underwear and jerked them down far enough to wiggle out of them. Her breasts swayed and the way his eyes darkened was heady. A tiny second of a strip tease and he'd grown even thicker.

He kissed the side of her mouth, then nibbled his way down her neck. His arms came around her and she arched against his hold.

When his lips closed around her nipple, she mewled. Good thing it was dark. She never made needy sounds like that. Her cheeks flushed, but the reason was no longer embarrassment. What he was doing with his tongue, combined with the scrape of his teeth, ignited her like a brush fire.

He switched his attention to the other side and the only thing she mourned was that his bent position kept him from pressing against her.

"Lucas, I need you now." She didn't want to find out if a girl could explode from not orgasming.

He straightened. His hair stuck out from where her hands had been running through it. His lips were parted and his eyes were glazed over and brimming with lust. "Get on the bed."

Her breath caught and a shiver ran over her body. Refraining from a frantic belly flop, she crawled over the rumpled covers, pushing them out of the way until she stretched across the fitted sheet.

He stared at her, but his expression wasn't one of rapt awe. Instead, he looked like he might bolt. Giving himself a shake, he grabbed a condom box from the nightstand. It fumbled in his grip and dropped to the floor.

"Shit." He stooped to get it. She watched, her radar going off. Something was wrong.

His fingers scrabbled at the top and he finally tore it open. Withdrawing the accordion strip, he dropped the empty box.

"Never been opened?" she teased.

He paused midrip. The condoms dangled in his hand. His gaze raked her body, but he drew back.

She propped herself on her elbows. "What's wrong?"

He looked down at the condoms, then back to her. His expression broke her heart. Tortured and uncertain.

"I don't… I haven't…"

She sat up, uncaring of how her stomach pooched. "Have you been with anyone since the divorce?"

The way his jaw tightened answered her question. "I haven't been with anyone but her."

Trina scooted to the edge of the bed. She'd never really thought about his sex life. He'd started dating Shaylee when he was young and then had married her. Since then, what had she thought? That he'd been sowing his wild oats? If he flirted with someone at the bar, she quit paying attention to him altogether. A few times, he'd even walked out with a woman, and yeah, she'd seethed inside, but hadn't she done the same thing with her hookups?

Only she'd gone home with them. Lucas had gone home alone?

"You've left with women before." Make-out sessions? She didn't want to think about it. His history was none of her business, but something was bothering him.

"I just walked them to their vehicle. When it came time to go further, I couldn't. Didn't want to." A troubled line creased his brow. "It's not just that." He shifted. His erection started to wane.

Trina stood. They had grown closer over the last few weeks, but what he was holding back was deeply personal. "It's okay, Lucas. You can tell me."

"She…" The man was tight, as rock-solid as a granite statue. Whatever he was holding in was going to split him at the seams if he didn't talk. "She had a lot of criticisms about my performance. I didn't make her happy. In bed." The hand holding the condoms hung limp at his side. "I understand if I ruined the mood and you don't want to do this. With me."

The image of perky little Shaylee with her perfect hair and designer clothes critiquing a vulnerable Lucas who only wanted to please her was disturbingly clear. Maybe one or the other lacked the skills of pleasure. Or maybe Shaylee hadn't cared to let Lucas try. It'd give her the upper hand, after all, a reason to shift the blame for their failing marriage to him.

But Lucas wasn't a guy who wouldn't try to please his wife. Trina suspected he had more skills than his bitch of an ex had given him credit for. The way he kissed drove her mindless.

She twined her arms around his neck. "Have you or have you not gotten me naked in your bedroom already?"

His was still like granite under her touch, but his cock twitched against her belly. "I have."

"Then why don't you fuck me and let me decide for myself."

"Lie down again," he said hoarsely. The sound of foil tearing echoed through the room.

LUCAS WAS GOING TO COMBUST. Trina resumed the position she'd been in and spread her legs like she knew that would be enough to break through his sudden case of insecurity.

"Trina." His groan was more reverence than pain.

He might relive the humiliation he'd just experienced one day, but desire pounded through his veins now, too strong to ignore. She wanted him to fuck her. *Let me decide for myself.*

It was the most thrilling test he'd ever taken. And one he didn't want to fail.

Rolling the condom on, he had to rely on muscle memory. It'd been a long time since he'd needed to don one, but mostly he couldn't take his eyes off her. The sexy vixen splayed across his bed was better than he could've fantasized.

And he'd fantasized. It'd been hard enough to sleep the

last month knowing she was living a hundred yards away. Now she was here.

"I want to taste you." He didn't recognize his own caveman voice.

She widened her knees and trailed her hand over her belly, heading toward—

He dropped on top of her and pinned her arm by her head. "This is for me tonight." She was taking a leap of faith with him and he was going to prove himself.

He pressed a kiss on her lips, then on each breast, licking a circle around her nipple and blowing across it. She squirmed under him.

Releasing her arm, he worked his way down her belly. His ex always complained that he took too long, but Trina wasn't complaining and she let him set the pace.

As soon as he reached her center, he wedged his shoulders between her thighs and licked through her fold. She bucked and moaned. It sounded good, so he kept going until he tongued her clit.

"Luuucasss."

He would smile, but he was too busy. The next several minutes were all a test. Of his stamina, which was at its limit, the brush of the bedding nearly too much. And of her response when he went slow. Or fast and rhythmic. How she gasped when he sucked on her.

Her hands tangled in his hair and she rocked against his tongue. He was having the best time of his life, but she needed more.

Teasing her entrance with a finger, he waited until she was close to begging before sliding inside. What would it be like if she came on his tongue?

Back to the test. She liked the steady slide in and out, and if one finger was good, two was even better.

She tightened around him, her hands twisting in his hair,

chanting his name until she went taut. Warmth flooded his hand but he didn't let up until she crested. Even then he didn't scramble away, but crawled up her body to hold her as she floated down.

"So far so good." Her hair was mussed as badly as his, and whatever lip color she'd put on earlier was long gone. Like she'd worn it just for him to lick off.

Hitching her leg over his arm, he pushed at her entrance but didn't fully seat himself. Was the multiple-orgasm thing bullshit? He didn't think so, but he'd never gotten the chance to try. "I want to get you off again."

She cocked her head and her smile was straight-up sarcastic. "No, please don't." She tilted her pelvis up, pushing him farther inside. "Do it."

This woman.

He plunged in. The instant he was surrounded by her wet heat, his balls tightened. No, dammit! He was going to impress her. He'd waited over two years to be with someone again and he wasn't going to blow his load in three seconds.

Grinding his jaw down, he slid out and back in. His entire body shook. Her heels dug into his ass and she'd wrapped her arms around his head and pulled him toward her.

Her lips at his neck were his undoing. His hips had a mind of their own. At least the latex saved him from coming in two pumps. He jacked in and out and she met him stroke for stroke. Soon, she was gasping and their bodies slapped together with greater force.

Nope. He wouldn't last. Wedging his hand between them, he rested his fingers on her swollen clit and changed his angle to hit the mysterious G-spot he'd read too much about.

She arched under him, his name on her lips. A guy could get addicted to that.

As soon as her walls clenched around him, he was done.

A roar ripped from his throat and he slammed inside, his

balls smacking against her. She was so tight around him, so fucking perfect, he couldn't move in more than short jerks as he climaxed.

The release was stronger than he'd ever experienced. Energy zinged up and down his spine like he'd been plugged into his electric fence.

He peaked but took his time coming down. Opening his eyes, he stared down at a flushed Trina. Her blush went from her cheeks, down her neck, and across her neckline.

"So?" He managed a lazy grin. "Made up your mind yet?"

IT WAS SO LATE, but this was one of those rare nights Trina didn't have to worry about time. She didn't have to gather up clothing and shove a guy out of her house. And since she was currently riding Lucas, he wasn't about to kick her out.

Strong hands dug into her waist.

She suspected Shaylee had used insults to dog Lucas. The man was a beast in bed. Unstoppable. Enthusiastic. And his stamina—admirable.

She wasn't sure about hers at the moment. Never had she orgasmed so many times in a twenty-four-hour period. Maybe if she counted the few times she got herself off, she could compare tonight to a month on her own. But those times were no comparison to Lucas filling her inside and out.

He was ruining her. Each time he touched her, he ruined her future with other men. Could anyone else make her feel this good, this desired?

Part of it was the way he looked at her, like he was in awe of everything she did. All she'd done was sit back and let him take charge. When he rolled over and settled her over his shaft, he'd taken control of the pace. And she'd let him. Because she liked it. A lot.

Just like she preened at how gorgeous he made her feel. Feminine. Desired. Damn near ethereal. With her past lovers, even with Pax, it had all been about the final rush. *You get me off, I'll get you off.* That was as far as it went.

Lucas worshipped her. Their "rest" between the first time and the next was him tasting every inch of her.

She should've gone home, but the way he made her feel was refreshing. She'd waited a long time to be treated like this.

He grunted and rolled up into her, allowing her to take over as he sucked at the tender skin of her breasts.

"You're so fucking wet," he said against her chest. "I can't get enough."

"I didn't think you'd be hard again so soon." Her voice was so breathy, so needy. She only sounded like that around him.

"It's my time to play." He brushed his hands up her back and cradled her close. They were hardly moving against each other, but her rocking was enough to stimulate the spot that wanted him the most.

He crushed his hips up, then growled when he couldn't get enough power. In a heartbeat, she was flipped on her back, her arms stretched along his above her head.

The kiss he gave her wasn't hurried. Slow and languid, he swept his tongue in her mouth, then matched the strokes to his thrusts.

She was pinned so that only her legs could move. Widening for him, she met him until their flesh slapped and their moans were the only noises in the room.

It wasn't long before her body tightened, gripping him, and she hurdled over the crest. This time was different than before. This one was gentle. No less satisfying, but the connection between them couldn't be denied.

He still anchored her hands to the mattress, but his head had sagged into the crook of her neck.

"Woman, you're gonna kill me."

Any other guy. Another guy called her "woman" and she'd jackknife off the bed and storm out. But the reverence in his voice only made her smile. "Are you saying there won't be a third time?"

His laughter tickled her neck, sending shivers skittering across her skin. He pulled back, that lopsided smile in place. "If you stayed over, hell yes there'd be a third time." Some of the humor died away. "But I know you have to get back before morning."

He didn't just crawl off her. He laid kisses across her body before he straightened. "Do you, uh, need to use the bathroom or something first?"

His awkward after-sex talk was endearing. "Sure."

"As long as you promise not to disappear when it's my turn in there."

She crossed her heart, but his gaze darkened on her pebbled nipples. "Eyes up here, buddy. Besides. I haven't told you my verdict. Remember?"

She'd jokingly said she needed more subject material and he'd made her come again.

Rolling off the bed, she sidled around him, but walked backward to the hallway.

He glanced over his shoulder. "See something you like?"

She let him see her smirk before she turned away. The man had a nice ass.

She finished in the bathroom, then dressed while he disappeared inside. Was this time different because he didn't want her to go?

Would he want to see her again? Or had he gotten her out of his system and was ready to take on single life?

The thought made her nauseated. Her mind churned like a four-wheeler in a mud hole, wheels spinning over the same questions, not getting anywhere. Would he want to see her again? Would he even want to *pretend* to see her again?

She didn't want to pretend. Not anymore.

The floor squeaked behind her. Great, she was standing in the middle of his small bedroom, facing the bed like a stalker. And she wanted to—she shuddered—*talk*.

"You still look good." From his purr, it was hard to tell they'd just had sex for the last couple of hours.

She faced him. "So do you."

Boxers rode low on his hips. He'd brushed his hair back but it was still ruffled like he'd used his hand to do it. She wanted to curl up on his bare chest and cuddle for the night. *Cuddle* wasn't in her vocabulary, but his sexuality was overpowering.

He grinned, but his gaze flickered away. He never got complimented over his looks.

"Lucas." She twisted her hands together. Talking wasn't her strong suit. Sharing feelings or being open even less so. She hadn't grown up in a touchy-feely household and she shunned all of it. But this was important—for him. "Any problems in the bedroom weren't about you. They were about her."

He scratched the back of his neck and stared at the bed. Was he going to reply? Had she overstepped her bounds? "Yeah." He dropped his hand. "I know that now. There were plenty of other issues, though."

"Didn't mean they were your fault." She'd guess there was equal blame at a minimum, or that Shaylee tipped the scales.

The smile he gave her was even. "I appreciate it, Tree-bee, but I don't want to end this night talking about the end of my marriage." He advanced and came to a stop, looming over her. It wasn't the intimidation tactic she usually experienced in the bar. "I want to end it with the taste of you on my lips."

He dipped his head and she rose to meet him. The kiss was slow, promising. And made it clear that talking about his past was off-limits.

For the first time in years, he was choosing her over Shaylee. He was choosing what they could feel together over the pain his ex had caused. So why didn't it feel like more of a victory?

CHAPTER 9

Lucas was bent over the hood of the Chevy when quick footsteps crunched the gravel behind him. "Lucas! Whatcha doing!"

He was smiling by the time he turned around. The pickup he'd thought was ready to sell had developed an oil leak. A bad seal and a worn gasket later, he was nearly finished. With the hot sun beating down on his garage and only a little wind making its way inside to cool him off, Brayden's enthusiasm was like a cold can of lemonade, which was now stocked in his beer fridge.

A week had gone by since the wedding. Trina had come over the following night, and a few more times throughout the week. He doubted Brayden suspected a thing, and Lucas was fine with that. There was no reason to lead the kid on. Lucas wouldn't be a replacement dad. Couldn't be if he wanted. Before he became a father, he wanted more financial security than fixing up and selling old vehicles his dad had left sitting in the field.

Until then, he wasn't any good to anyone.

Lucas grabbed a rag, wiping his hands. The kid was

running his own toy truck on the ground, crouched so his little bony knees stuck up close to his shoulders. The toy truck would probably sell for as much as this old one. "Brayman. What are you up to today?"

"Nothing. Mom's working."

"Grandma D know you're here?"

Brayden shook his head. "She's in town getting parts. Sarah said it was okay to run over here, but that if I was bothering you, I had to get my butt back home."

That sounded like Sarah. "I'll let her know you're total trouble, but I don't mind if you stay."

His days could be long and lonely, especially since he no longer had an employee. He didn't see Davina or Sarah nearly enough to stave off the feeling that it was him against the world. Truthfully, it was part of the reason he looked forward to visiting Dad. The comfort of routine, the need to connect with his father, but also the chance to speak to other humans.

He needed to get a dog. His barn cats wanted nothing to do with him unless he was dumping kibble in their dishes. They were ferocious enough to keep even skunks away, but...maybe a dog wouldn't hurt.

"How's your mom's job coming?" Lucas knew perfectly well. Since they'd slept together, Trina had opened up in so many ways. She laughed about Brayden's antics, the pride ringing in her voice. And excitement swirled around her as she talked about everything she was learning. Her training was nearly done and she was—he never thought he'd say this about her—*gushing* about how she looked forward to starting work in the center.

"Good." Plastic wheels pinged over rocks as he made figure eights in the dirt.

"I think I need a dog."

Brayden's head popped up, his eyes bright. "What are you gonna name it?"

Lucas crossed to the garage sink. "I might not have to worry about a name. Let me wash up and talk to Sarah." He dried his hands and pulled out his phone. Hitting Sarah's number, he jumped right to his request. "Sarah? Can Brayden come with me and help me pick out a dog?"

Sarah's laugh cackled over the line. "He's going to want every dog you see."

"Think Trina will mind?"

"Didn't you ask her last night?"

He cleared his throat. They weren't making any announcements about their non-status or how their little pretend relationship was sort of not pretend. Sarah wasn't going to go screaming it around town, Davina either, but he felt like he should say something. He was sleeping with the woman's daughter. "About that—"

"Relax, Lucas. It's none of my business. You two are adults. D and I aren't sitting on the porch with shotguns because you're dating our girl." Her and Davina rocking on the porch, ball caps pulled down low, eyeballing him as he walked Trina home was enough to make a guy's knees shake. Not that Trina would tolerate her moms in her business, or that she would let him walk her home.

They weren't dating. That was the issue. They were sleeping together—only there was no sleep involved. Just a lot of nudity and the yelling of his name—which he wouldn't get tired of anytime soon.

Sex with Trina was an epiphany. The act could be about mutual pleasure and not about control and guilt-inducing tactics that could later be used to get him to agree to anything, like spending his hard-earned money on a trip to Mexico when he really needed to upgrade his irrigation system.

"Just have Brayden run over and grab his booster seat and get him back by five. She'll worry if he's not home when she gets back."

His girl was protective of her boy.

His girl. Trina was Trina. Her own self-made woman. She didn't count on him for anything. And that was for the best.

He passed the instructions on to Brayden. The boy ran off with a whoop.

His phone buzzed, and his smile died when he saw Shaylee's name scrawled across the screen. Why the hell couldn't she leave him alone?

It was like she sensed he was emotionally moving on, finally, and had upped whatever game she was playing. Call me, please.

That was all she ever said. A message along those lines, or "we need to talk," or "please don't be like this, Lucas. Talk to me."

He had nothing left to say. The night he'd crashed to his knees and begged her not to leave him was as fresh as a festering wound.

He'd thought he'd be married forever, have a love as strong as his parents. Mom had lost Dad, not in body, but in spirit, and it had destroyed her. The doctors hadn't said the aneurysm was caused by stress, but did they have to?

Yeah, he needed the dog as a distraction.

He shoved his phone back in his pocket and stomped out of the garage to where his working vehicle was parked by the house. Brayden was already flying back from the tree row, bulky booster seat hugged to his chest.

"Hop in."

Brayden jabbered all the way to town. Lucas only had to fill in with "uh-huh" and "really" here and there, but the conversation was a rainbow in a depressing day that had started with a mailbox full of bills.

"Where are we?" Brayden asked as Lucas pulled up at the building attached to the police department.

"The pound. Some of these are lost dogs, but some don't have a home or anyone looking for them. I thought we'd try here first."

Inside, the middle-aged attendant with a nametag that read *Paola* brought them back to a room full of kennels. Cats in smaller kennels lined one wall, and the dogs were in cages closer to the fenced-in yard for potty breaks.

"Don't be shoving your fingers in every cage. Your mom wants me to return you with all your fingers and toes." Lucas tried to be authoritative, but Brayden was dissolving into fits of laughter from the fluffy little dog that was licking him.

Lucas kept his eye out for a dog that could not only tolerate being outside, but would love it.

A steady thump drew his attention to a cage in the corner.

"That one was found running in the country," Paola said. "We think his owners moved and left him behind. No tags, but well behaved. He responds to commands."

"Do you know what breed he his?" Lucas drifted closer. The dog's tongue lolled out and the tail kept a steady *thump, thump*.

"A mix of some sort, but there's definitely retriever in him. We call him Gus."

Deep brown eyes regarded him. Lucas put his hand to the bars. Gus was on him in a second, soft licks sweeping his fingers.

"Um…" Paola stepped to the side. "So we found Gus with this guy." The cage next to Gus held a smaller dog. Lucas wasn't familiar with animals, but he'd guess it was a heeler of some sort. That dog was pressed against the bars, straining to check out the humans Gus was focused on. "They're really close. Like, Buster here whines when Gus goes outside without him."

Two dogs? He'd always had a dog growing up, and he lived on a farm, but feeding two active dogs wouldn't be cheap. Still…his place was really quiet.

"Are they outdoor dogs?"

"If they didn't start that way, they had to be after they were abandoned. But, yes, they love it outside."

Davina and Sarah's old dog had passed away last year. Neither of them would mind Gus or Buster as long as they weren't cattle chasers. But he'd have time to train them. "All right. Call me a sucker. I'll take them both. Hear that, Brayden?" He looked around. Brayden wasn't next to him.

Shit. Losing a kid among stray animals was just what he'd do.

Spinning around, he found Brayden huddled in a corner. One of the cat cages hung open and in Brayden's lap was a mound of orange- and white-striped fluff.

Paola laughed, acting like it was inevitable that kid would've found that cat. "And that is Mr. Whiskers. Real original, I know." She spoke quietly to Lucas. "He was supposed to be euthanized a year ago, but the dang cat purrs up a storm when you so much as look at him. He may be my secret project. I have three cats at home and Mr. Whiskers here doesn't get along with other animals."

"Too bad I'm taking two dogs already."

"Oh, he's an indoor cat." Paola pinned him with a direct brown stare. "You don't have any indoor pets, do you?"

Trina slid out of her car, popping the hood before she shut the door.

"Something wrong?" Mom called from across the yard.

"I think so." She wouldn't be able to tell by looking under the hood, but it made her feel less powerless. "I think it's the transmission."

"It's old enough." Mom came to a stop by her and they both glowered at the dusty engine.

"The RPMs were revving and I had to stop and start it twice before it acted normal." Trina sighed. If it was the transmission, and it probably was, she couldn't do a damn thing about it. "I hope it'll last for a few months so I can save up to fix it."

Mom brushed a hand through her trimmed brunette hair. Gray strands glinted in the sun. "I hate to see you dump that much money on an old beater."

She wasn't the only one. "It'll cost as much as a whole semester of school." And it'd mean she'd have to work all through nursing school if she had to dig into the money she planned to save up while working the next year. Mooing from the distant pasture drifted through the otherwise quiet yard. "Where's Brayden?"

"He spent the afternoon with Lucas." Mom chuckled. "I think Brayden is going to be over there a lot more now."

"Why?" Brayden had been with Lucas most of the day? Did Lucas mind?

"Oh, go over there and you'll see." Mom's smile faded. "Are you two...serious?"

Trina crossed her arms. Hadn't she been asking herself similar versions of the same question? They'd only been sleeping together a week, but they'd fallen into an easy routine. What they hadn't done was go on another date, or talked about going on another date. Neither had they eaten a meal together, or hell, even talked about anything deeper than which room to have sex in.

No, *he* never talked about anything deeper. She couldn't seem to keep her mouth shut.

"Not really," she finally answered.

Mom nodded once. "Good. He's a good guy, but Shaylee really did a number on him and I don't want to see you hurt because of it."

"So…?" Mom didn't think they should be dating? Or that she couldn't possibly be enough to fill up the void Shaylee had left?

"Take it slow is all I'm saying. I want to be the biggest supporter of you two, but he's been different since the divorce. Quieter. Even through all that shit with his dad, he never lost his optimism, his drive to keep going. But that wife of his chewed him up and spat him out on the side of the road. Then did a little dance on his remains." Mom glared toward Lucas's property. "Never did like her."

"You know I'm not one to go diving into long-term relationships."

"But we both know he's different. And you act different with him."

Trina rolled her eyes and was transported back fifteen years when Mom had given her the boy talk. "Because we grew up together. Maybe he's just comfortable. We used to be friends." Before he'd decided that she wasn't dating material.

"Just take a mom's word of warning, will ya, kiddo?" Mom patted her shoulder. "Good luck getting your son home."

Her snicker while walking away was almost sinister. Trina narrowed her eyes on the white house cresting above the treetops. Time to find out what Mom had meant.

She'd just cleared the tree row when she saw exactly what Mom had meant. Two dogs frolicked at Lucas's feet. A treat bag dangled from his hand and he took turns giving commands and rewarding the dogs.

His words floated on the wind toward her. "Good job, Gus."

The dogs both started for her, but a word from Lucas stopped them.

This was a story she had to hear. "You're with my kid for one afternoon and you let him talk you into not one dog, but two?"

Lucas's grin warmed her more than the high evening sun. "Between him and the pound attendant, I didn't stand a chance." He jutted his chin toward the house. "The real kicker's inside."

She veered off toward the house. The dogs could wait. Her motherly instincts demanded she check on Brayden first. He didn't go to other people's places often. The kid didn't have a lot of close friends and when he was at Pax's, Trina wondered if he was treated more as an afterthought.

"Brayden?"

"Here." He was stretched across the couch, a slumbering orange tabby on his belly.

"What the—" She barked out a laugh. "You talked Lucas into a cat? He has several outside."

"Mr. Whiskers is an indoor cat and nobody wanted him because he doesn't do well with other animals."

She pointed outside, her smile wide. "There are other animals here." Her gaze landed on a half-empty box of litter and bags of cat supplies. "He's such a sucker."

"That's what he told Paola."

She couldn't quit smiling. The cat wore a blissed-out expression and her son was the most relaxed she'd ever seen him. No toys. No games.

"Mr. Whiskers?" She could picture Lucas stumbling into the kitchen, wearing nothing but his boxers as he dug out the Meow Mix, calling for his new cat.

"Lucas said he's not going to change the name. The pound

said they didn't care, but they made him promise to bring Mr. Whiskers back to visit."

The image of Lucas brandishing a portly orange tabby in front of gruff pound workers snaked through her mind. He was so far removed from the sloppy drunk farmer in the bar.

"Let's hear it," Lucas said from behind her.

She jumped and spun around. He leaned against the doorframe, his arms crossed and his eyes glinting with humor. She put her hand on her chest. "Why, Lucas Herman Peterson, I would never comment on the accumulation of three animals when you probably weren't planning on getting one this morning."

Clamping her mouth shut, she fought her furious blush. Today had been an extra caffeine day because she'd left his bed in the early hours of the morning. And no, he hadn't mentioned any plans to grow his menagerie.

He smirked. "Your moms are going to help me acclimate the dogs to the horses and cattle for the rest of the week. I have them leashed for now." He pushed off the door. "Anyway. I'm going to run to town and have dinner with Dad. I just wanted to let you know you don't have to rush off." He nodded toward Brayden gently stroking the cat. "Good luck."

"I stopped by your dad's room after work. I didn't know if you'd been there yet." Since Lucas and Marilyn were Herman's only visitors, she made sure to stop by a couple times a week.

"I had to work on the Chevy."

Which reminded her— "Know anything about transmissions?"

He snorted. "Enough to know that I can't fix them. The car I pulled out of the pasture before the pickup was a waste. I sold it for scrap."

She winced. "I hope that's not my car's fate." The distance between them felt like a chasm. She couldn't give him the not-so-quick goodbye kiss she normally did in the middle of the night. "We'll see you later?"

He gave her that heated look that incited toe-curling memories. "Later."

She tried not to think how natural it felt to hang out in his living room with her son, or how she'd like to do it more. One thing she couldn't ignore—he'd never invited her or Brayden over, never mentioned the option.

They weren't dating. They weren't even pretending to date anymore. So where did they go from here?

CHAPTER 10

hy'd August have to be so hot?

Lucas idled the tractor into place by Davina's shop. Windrows stretched in wavy lines where he'd cut and raked pasture grass. He'd help Davina and Sarah bale before it was supposed to rain at the end of the week. And then it'd be harvest season and he'd be married to his combine.

At least that marriage wasn't as hard on his ego as his previous one had been.

Once a week, Shaylee sent a message. He had no idea what she wanted to talk about, but his gut told him that it'd be nothing good for him to hear—and he'd heard a lot in their time together. So maybe it was experience talking.

Davina came out of the shed. She was a tinier, older version of her daughter. Same straight, short hair. Same guarded look in her eyes. But Trina's perma-scowl came from her dad.

"Did Trina ask you to come with us tonight?" Davina asked.

Trina was graduating from her CNA course. And yes, she

had. He wanted to go cheer her on, but with harvest looming and hay that still needed to be stacked, he only had a small window to get the pickup cleaned up and sold.

Just a few more tweaks and it'd be running smoothly. He only owed his new buddy, Jesse, a half a freezer of vacuum-sealed chicken for the oil leak that wasn't a simple bad seal like he'd first thought. That chicken he'd get from Davina and Sarah for helping cut hay, though Jesse would refuse it if he found out.

So Lucas wouldn't mention it.

"She did," he replied, "but I have some work to finish up."

"Catch us for dinner after the ceremony?"

Trina claimed the ceremony wasn't a big deal. *Just a small gathering where we get our certificates.* But the way her face radiated excitement each time she mentioned it meant the small ceremony was a big deal to her, and he wasn't going to show with dirt on his boots and sweat soaking his hat.

"I might be done in time. Just tell Trina to let me know when and where if she wants me there." He wasn't about to invite himself into any of her family time. She'd chided Brayden the other day for not finishing his chores because he'd been playing with the dogs all day.

Davina's look lingered on him like she wanted to say more, but she only nodded. "Thanks for your help today. We weren't sure we'd get this all cut once we heard they were predicting storms."

"Don't mention it." They always paid him, whether in money or goods or returning the favor during harvest. "Now you're gonna be sending your baby off to college," he teased.

"She's sending herself. You know she'd gnaw her arm off before she lets me help." Davina peeked around the yard even though Trina was in town for her final day of training. "Between you and me, I'm surprised she took me up on my invite back home. But I'm not above admitting that I'm glad she's staying in Moore for school."

He wasn't either, if it even mattered. The other night when she'd come over after Brayden had gone to bed, she'd pored over her fall schedule and planned when she could work and study. He'd pulled up his seeding records to have something productive to do.

Her days would be packed. Full of learning, working, and raising her kid. His days would be the same. They'd be in the same town, but she'd be miles ahead of anywhere he'd gotten.

"We'll see you later, then." Davina strode away and Lucas crossed through the yard and trees. As he cleared through to his place, a glint of metal caught his eye.

He knew that car. He'd bought that car—and paid it off in the divorce.

Shaylee was walking down the front steps of his place, his dogs keeping pace with her. Her navy-blue scrubs were looser than she used to wear them. He assumed she still worked as a dental hygienist for the dentist she'd left him for, but he tried not to care.

He was transported back to when he'd done this walk before. Coming back from helping the neighbors, anticipation at spending a quiet evening with his wife as she returned from a long day of work.

When had it all changed? When had the wattage of her smile dimmed until she'd stared at him like she did now? Her full lips were pressed into a troubled line. Her hand shaded her eyes as she warily regarded him.

"Shaylee," he said as he got close to where she waited by her car.

He couldn't help the part of him that wanted to excuse himself and rush inside to shower. Dust covered him from head to toe, his pants had a hole by the front right pocket, and he smelled like a combo of burned oil and fresh-cut grass.

But she knew what it was like to be married to a farmer. It was why she'd left.

She folded her arms across herself. There was something different about her, but he couldn't pinpoint it. Her face was fuller. She glowed. Shaylee being beautiful wasn't different, though.

"Gus, sit. Buster, sit." The dogs listened. They were more eager than him to find out why she was here.

Her soft blue gaze flicked to the patient animals. "You have dogs."

"A cat too." When she looked toward the barn where his cats usually resided, he amended, "An indoor cat."

"Oh. I'm allergic to cats."

"I know." How many times had he questioned himself as to the real reason why Mr. Whiskers now lived with him?

She frowned, but it didn't seem aimed toward him. "I've been trying to reach you."

"I know."

She knew he was ignoring her. He filled to the brim with questions. Why was she here? Why had she been so unhappy? Had he really not satisfied her in bed? Was Trina right, had it been a control tactic?

But this wasn't the time. That had come and gone. Like before, he wasn't sure the answers would help more than they hurt.

"Whaddya need?" he asked, impatient to drop the hammer that hovered over his head.

"I wanted to see how you were doing."

No, that wasn't it. Why she wasn't coming out with it, he didn't know. He spread his arms out. "Same old. You remember how August is."

Can't you quit early one night? I thought we could get away this weekend. All the other people I work with take big vacations in August.

Lines of tension radiated around her eyes. She closed them and inhaled. "I've missed this. Quiet."

"Nothing but the birds." It used to be their joke when they were first married. Young and stupid, living out here like they each knew what they were doing. Until she'd wised up and wanted someone who had his shit together—and the financial means to do it.

A faint smile played over her lips. "Nothing but the birds." She tilted her head, the glossy ponytail she kept her flaxen hair in while she worked swinging over her shoulder. "How's your dad?"

"Same." That summed up all his answers. How was the money situation? Same. How was the family treating him? Same. How was the outlook of his family business? Same. Did he still fear keeping a roof over his dad's head?

That one had changed. He worried more.

He didn't inquire about her. If she said life was shit and she regretted leaving, he'd feel like crap, and more than a little guilty. Did he regret his failure of a marriage? Yes. But he didn't wish to go back to that place. Their early days had been full of youthful optimism. Those last days were the truest either of them had lived and he wouldn't go back to wearing rose-colored glasses. Authenticity hurt, but he was getting by.

Which brought him back to this non-conversation. "Shaylee, what'd you come all the way out here to tell me?"

She hugged herself tighter and met his gaze. "I'm pregnant."

He rocked back on his heels like she'd pushed him. "Oh. Oh, wow."

When they were first married, *I don't know if I ever want kids, Lucas,* had eventually turned to *I am not having any babies while we have an adult man to take care of. Do you think I want to bring a kid into this world, living paycheck to paycheck like we do? My paycheck.*

His throat grew tight. "Congrats." He wanted a fucking award for being a reasonable adult. "I'm happy for you."

"Lucas—"

"You don't have to explain to me. I mean it. Congrats." He tore his gaze away. The dogs scooted to his feet, their tails whispering against the gravel of his driveway.

"I do, though. I know what I said when we talked about kids."

When *he'd* talked about kids. "No, you don't. I'm sure a dentist brings in more than I do. A nice, secure home. That's what you wanted for your kids."

"Yeah." She dragged her lower lip between her teeth. He hated that he knew her well enough to know something bothered her. "It was an accident."

"Oh." That didn't make her news any better. She'd said sleeping with the dentist was an accident too.

"That's why he proposed."

He bobbed his head. Really, he just wanted her to go. He wanted to go inside, clean up, and veg on the couch with the revenge cat he'd rescued.

His phone vibrated in his pocket. Now he knew it wasn't Shaylee.

He was about to say he needed to go for some made-up reason he couldn't quite identify, but she wasn't done with him. "I wanted to talk to you myself. I thought maybe Trina said something."

A flood of ice water splashed through his veins. "Trina? Why?"

"Well, I thought maybe she noticed when she served me at Barley 'n' Hops. I heard she's living next door again."

"No. Trina didn't mention anything." His voice was hard.

Trina had known? Suspected? Why hadn't she said anything? *Hey, your ex that never wanted kids turns out to never have wanted* your *kids. She's pregnant.* "Congrats, Shaylee. Take care."

He stalked toward his house. The dogs tailed him, but he didn't look at them. He didn't look back as the bang of a car door resonated across his yard and Shaylee drove off.

His phone buzzed again. He withdrew it.

Details of the CNA graduation and where Trina and her family were eating afterword scrolled across the screen.

He entered his house, dumped the phone on the nearest shelf, and stalked toward the shower.

Nope. He wouldn't be celebrating anything tonight.

"I KNOW it's only the beginning," Trina said to one of her classmates, Janie. "But I'm still thrilled this phase is done."

"Oh, I know." Janie twisted her hands. She was a nervous girl. Maybe that was why Trina liked her. She didn't hide her nerves and Trina could live vicariously through her hand wringing. "It seems like such a long journey, but we can tick off one hurdle."

Trina nodded and took a drink of her punch. The cozy reception was nearly over, and then she'd meet her moms and Brayden at the restaurant. Janie worked at the hospital, but she planned to start college classes in the fall with Trina and apply for the LPN program in the spring.

As she chatted, she checked her phone. No reply from Lucas.

Janie sighed. "I'd better get to work. The night shift awaits."

"Just remember: I'll be there to elbow you awake in algebra next month."

"I'm counting on it."

Trina thanked her instructors and was grateful Marilyn's presence was limited. The cool looks she gave Mom worried Trina. She couldn't afford personal matters derailing her college plans.

She found Mom. "Hey. Have you heard from Lucas?"

"Not since this afternoon."

Trina's heart sank. Like she'd told Janie, this graduation was symbolic. The future she'd planned for was happening. She was moving forward, and she wanted Lucas to be here.

"He was pretty busy," Mom said. "Maybe he just can't hear the phone. Should we head over to the restaurant?"

Trina made a quick decision. "Gimme a half hour. Let Brayden order an appetizer."

"Going to check on Lucas." There was no censure in Mom's statement, just concern.

A couple of minutes later, Trina was flying down the gravel stretch to her place. She wasn't a woman who chased men, but having this dinner felt empty without him.

She pulled into his drive. The dogs were there. The garage door was shut. He wasn't working on the Chevy then. She parked and jogged to his door. Adjusting the skirt to the same dress she wore to the wedding with one hand, she knocked with the other.

Lucas opened the door and slung his arm along the side. The screen door stayed shut between them. His expression was pounded, like he'd gotten into a fight and just hadn't bruised yet.

"Did you get my text?" she asked.

He let out a slow exhale. His hair was wet and he was wearing basketball shorts and a T-shirt. Freshly showered. But his eyes were tired. Sad. "Yeah. Sorry. I can't make it tonight."

That's it? Over a month of sleeping together and he was blowing her off? "I see. Are you feeling okay?"

"Not really." He rubbed his eyes. "Did you…uh… Did you know that Shaylee was pregnant?"

The thump of her heart echoed between her ears. It was her day, a big day to her, and he was asking about his ex? "No. Not really. She ordered a cranberry spritzer when she was in the bar a while ago and I wondered. But not for long because she's not someone I want to waste mental energy on." She'd done too much of that years ago.

He watched her, his expression guarded. Then his gaze dropped to her dress, appreciation in his eyes. She hated how quickly she latched on to his approval. "How was graduation?"

"Good. We're going out to eat now." She swallowed hard. After having driven all this way, she wanted to give him one more chance. "Want to come with?"

"I'm not really presentable." Genuine regret passed over his face. "I'm sorry."

"Sure." She pivoted to get to her car, disappointment soaking her like an early morning mist.

The screen door opened. "Trina." He closed a hand around her upper arm. "I'm sorry." She softened under him, and under the tangible pain in his voice. "She came out here to tell me and it kind of fucked me up."

A few more minutes wouldn't hurt. She gently pushed him inside. "Are you doing okay?"

His head hung and he slouched against the wall by the door. "Yeah. It's just…" He shook his head and looked up. "She didn't want kids. With me."

"She's an idiot." Trina knew without asking that it was an issue Shaylee had thrown in Lucas's face often, one that she had twisted to make Lucas suffer.

"Yeah." He drew her into him. "I'm happy for you though. I didn't want to drag down your day."

But he had. Yet, she tipped her head back to capture his kiss. He'd been upset and wanted to be alone. She understood. And she was willing to forgive. This time.

So unlike her.

A low growl vibrated through his chest. He hugged her to him and spun her around. Her body responded instantly to his touch. He'd learned quickly, intuitively, what she liked, and at the moment, they both needed to feel better. The way he was hurting bothered her.

Twining her legs around him, she appreciated the freedom of the dress and how easy it was to shove her underwear to the side. He pushed her against the wall and with one hand, he shoved down his shorts.

"Fuck," he murmured against her lips. "The condoms are in my bedroom."

They'd had this talk before. She was on birth control, but a condom created more than a physical barrier between them and they'd kept using one.

She wedged her hand between them, gripped his hot shaft, and positioned him. Without hesitation, he rocked inside, coating himself in her more and more until he was seated fully. There was no break.

He thrust and she clung to him, their mouths clashing. The urgency, combined with the charged emotions between them, propelled her to an early climax. As elation washed over her, it turned into an out-of-body experience. Like she was watching herself come over him, and him pinning her against the wall. Him stiffening with his release inside of her, filling her with warmth that didn't reach the most important part of her.

A quickie like this should be erotic. Most of the time, sex for her was a release, a way to get off and feel temporarily close to someone without the bullshit of a doomed relationship. She hadn't realized how different it'd been with Lucas until now, when it was like all the other times before him. Mutual orgasms. *I scratch your itch and you scratch mine.*

Then he dropped a lingering kiss on the corner of her mouth. "I shouldn't have kept you from your celebration. I really am proud of you."

She gazed into his warm brown eyes. Maybe it had been her imagination. "Thanks."

Untangling herself from him, she lowered her legs. Her whole body was shaky, unsteady, and the feeling spread to her mind.

"I hate to leave, but…" She had to run home and clean up. Staying here longer wasn't an option. She needed to go home for a minute and soak up the quiet to organize her thoughts, to remember why she didn't do relationships.

"Are you coming back?" He was still cradling her, her back against the wall. How did he do this? At the times she should walk, he made her feel special. He treated her like she was special.

"I'll come over tonight. I don't work until Monday." Except for a couple of shifts she'd picked up at the bar, but she could mention it later. People were waiting on her, and she was missing her own party for Lucas.

Who was wearing his PJs and hadn't planned on going.

Extracting herself, she slipped out the door with a small smile, but on the way to her car, her lower lip trembled.

She sucked it in between her teeth. No. After her dad had walked out and never called again, and after Pax had told her that he needed to be free to answer the call of his muse, she'd refused to shed tears over any man.

But she couldn't stop the one that escaped and rolled a blistering streak down her cheek.

CHAPTER 11

"Thanks, Sarah." Lucas hopped down from the combine. The sun was still up, but going down earlier and earlier now that it was late September.

Sarah had already parked the grain truck. She had run loads to the silo while he'd run the combine. They were doing the same routine from last year. He helped them harvest their silage fields, and when it came time to bring in his soybeans and corn, Sarah changed her route from the silo to the grain bins. "Don't mention it."

"I have to. I don't know how I'd do this without you." They were more like partners than separate entities. Two aging ranchers and a single farmer. With Sarah and Davina's help, he stayed viable. He'd like to think it was likewise, but no.

Sarah smiled, her gray eyes crinkling. The ponytail that stuck out of the back of her hat was streaked with a brighter gray than her eyes. "That's what neighbors do. Besides, we'll see you when it's time to work cattle." She gave him a wave as she walked off.

Working cattle took all of two days, but he appreciated her effort at downplaying the level of help he needed.

He checked his phone. Still no message from Trina. She was deep into her studies, and he almost never saw her.

He sent a message. Coming over tonight?

A few minutes later, her reply hit. No, I'm at the bar until late.

Lucas scowled. She hadn't mentioned picking up a shift. Last night when she'd asked what he was going to do with his Friday evening, he'd laughed and said he had a hot date with his combine.

A couple of times, she'd mentioned going out for supper again, but unless there was a set of golden arches outside, he had to save his money. The damn pickup hadn't sold yet. Three people who'd looked at it had lowballed him with their offers. There were several years under the hood, but he was still selling below its standard asking price. Then there'd been the lookers who wasted his time and theirs.

Another guy was coming to check it out Sunday. He wanted a farm-truck-slash-runaround-vehicle for his teen. This one would be perfect, but Lucas didn't want to get his hopes up. Except he needed the money by the end of the month. So his hopes were already too high.

She was at the bar. He made good time today. He could use a night out and afford one beer.

Running through the shower, he finished in record time and tossed on a clean pair of jeans and a T-shirt. Digging his nice boots out of the closet, he frowned at them. A layer of dust covered the toes. He brushed each boot off on a sweater hanging above him. When was the last time he'd worn these?

He'd planned to for Trina's ceremony, but he hadn't gone.

He couldn't escape feeling like he'd let her down. She hadn't said anything. And there was the blistering-hot episode against the wall that he was now squatting by.

But things hadn't been the same since. She didn't chatter as openly as she used to. It could be school. She was taking a heavy load and working several evenings and weekends, plus taking a shift here and there at the bar.

The wedding. That was the last time he'd worn the boots. Also a blistering memory. That night could've been life changing if he'd had the money to do anything about it. Before that night, he might've moped around the house for a month after the baby bomb Shaylee had dumped on him.

He straightened and stepped into his boots.

He was at Barley 'n' Hops within minutes. Driving through the lot, he spotted her car parked in a middle row. Usually, she parked by the bar's back exit with the other coworkers and they all left together. He could park close to her, but if she was closing the bar, he couldn't stay. Tomorrow would be another long day and he'd have to get a decent night's sleep or risk falling asleep at the tractor wheel.

As he entered, flashes of memory assaulted him. Seemed to be the night for all his failings to plague him. Those times he'd gotten sloppy drunk, Trina had handled his sorry ass. But the real risk of losing his farm had dropped a stopper in that leaky bucket. That and the shame of making an ass of himself in front of her. Everyone else thought he was a loser, but she knew the real him. It was why he was drawn to her. The only person in the world who knew what he'd once been like, the potential he'd had, before life had tossed curveball after fastball at him.

She grounded him in a way he'd never missed until now.

The familiar smells of beer and greasy bar food assaulted him. He scanned behind the long wood bar. No Trina. Maybe she was working the floor.

He sauntered in. If she was working the floor, he could sit by the pool tables and maybe pick up a game with someone.

He was in danger of wandering in circles when he finally

spotted her. Sitting. Two half-empty bottles of beer were on the table between her and a young woman he didn't recognize.

At the bar. Not *working* at the bar.

Well, now what should he do? He didn't want to infringe on her night out. But he'd only come here to see her.

The woman she was with lifted her gaze, a frown marring her features. She said a few words to Trina.

Trina looked over her shoulder, alarm in her eyes, but humor immediately infused them. He must look like a damn creeper, stalking through the bar, laser focused on her.

He grinned and Trina's friend relaxed. When he reached them, he leaned on the back of her chair. "Sarah said you were at the bar. I thought you were working."

A shadow flickered across Trina's face and was gone, her smile in place. Had he imagined it? "I thought I should take a night off."

"Good." He shouldn't be surprised that she had friends he didn't know about, but she worked too hard to meet people. He stuck his hand out to introduce himself. "Lucas. Nosy neighbor."

Trina shifted, but he couldn't see her expression while he reached across the table.

The woman gave his hand a polite squeeze. "Janie. Bossy classmate."

"She orders me around." Trina laughed. " 'Flashcards, Trina. Turn the TV off when you study, Trina. Make sure you go to bed early, Trina.' "

He could help with one of those three things—though it'd be hard. She got to bed late because she was between his sheets. Or on the counter. Or spread across his table.

He cleared his throat and stood back. "I won't intrude on your girls' night."

"Wait. You can take my seat. I have to get to work." Janie

downed her drink. It was a root beer bottle, not beer. She gave him a sheepish smile. "If I don't socialize before work, it doesn't happen."

She left with promises to meet up for study time between classes. Lucas slid into her vacated seat. Trina eyed him, a slight tilt to her head.

"What?"

"I thought you weren't doing anything tonight."

He reached into his wallet and withdrew a ten-dollar bill. "I can have ten bucks' worth of fun." He leaned forward. "But I've been having a whole lot of fun for free."

A blush stained her cheeks. Always a major victory when he got Trina Hart to blush. "Well, maybe I want to have fun outside of your house, and before midnight."

He was about to make another innuendo, but one of Trina's old coworkers stopped to take his order and chat with Trina. The man's nametag read *Loel* and he looked about ten years older than her. He asked Trina about school and acted genuinely thrilled for her.

A customer called his name. Loel nodded toward the guy but kept his attention on Trina. "We need to meet for coffee sometime."

Lucas tensed, his gaze narrowed on Loel. Was the man hitting on Trina in front of him?

What would he do if Loel was? Would Trina allow him to call her his girlfriend?

"Sounds fun. I have a long break between two classes Wednesday mornings."

Loel ducked his head. "Great. Shoot me a message. As long as I didn't close the night before, I'm game." He looked at Lucas. "What'll you have, man?"

"Bud." The word came out curt. He wasn't feeling like anything right now. He'd planned a night working or on his couch, but Trina was in high demand. He should be happy for her, but it was getting drowned in his self-pity and circumspection.

When Loel left, Trina studied him. "Something bothering you?"

So many things he could say ran through his mind, but he stuck on the fact that they'd never talked about being exclusive or official. "Should it?"

"Loel has worked here longer than me. We're friends." She took a slow drink, her steady gaze never leaving him.

He nodded and drummed his fingers on the table. The urge to act like a jealous boyfriend was hard to resist. But the theme of the night seemed to be memories.

We're just coworkers, Lucas. I can be friends with coworkers.

The office went out for drinks. I didn't mean to be so late.

I don't love you anymore, Lucas.

Like Trina had read his thoughts, she explained, "He's divorced and has been dating someone for the last two years. He also has a girl Brayden's age and an older son. We've met for coffee before to talk about kids and work, and we've had plenty of opportunities to get together if we were interested. We're not interested."

"You don't have to explain." He wanted her to, but he was mature enough to know she didn't have to. He was also adult enough to know he had no claim on her. She was going places, maybe not literally, but figuratively.

"I felt like I should."

He clenched his jaw and looked away. "Well, you don't."

A flash of hurt passed through her eyes. Did she want more? He had nothing to offer and she hadn't mentioned any deep desires to be in a relationship. "What changed your mind about coming out tonight?"

If she was moving on from coffee with Loel, then he'd hop on that train in a blink. "Sarah and I got done earlier than planned."

"Have you eaten yet?"

He shook his head and tapped the ten. "Eating out isn't in the budget."

"But beer is?" On cue, Loel appeared with his drink. "Can we get a plate of nachos?"

"Sure thing." Loel pocketed the money, dropping his change on the table. "Jalapenos?"

Trina lifted a brow toward him.

"Whatever the lady wants." She was right to stuff food into him. He should've thought about eating before he came for a drink. One beer should be equal to water for him, but he hadn't put food into his belly for hours on top of being outside all day.

"Is that why you quit drinking? Money?"

Yes. And no. Was there a way to answer without sounding like a guy who didn't have his shit together? "I woke up one morning, hungover as hell, and went to work. I had this pounding headache as I was fiddling with an auger when I lost my balance."

Trina sucked in a breath and automatically checked his arms, like they might've suddenly gone missing from that near auger accident a year ago.

"Yeah. It was dumb luck that I didn't lose a limb." Or worse.

If his hand got caught up in the auger and took his arm, or trapped him, there was no one around to help. Davina and Sarah could've been sitting in their living room and not heard him yell.

Who would've been around to pay his bills, much less his dad's?

He didn't have to fill in the rest. Trina would know the repercussions of getting hurt. Her moms had the same worries. All ranchers and farmers did. But unlike Davina and Sarah, he didn't have anyone next to him.

~

THE NIGHT WAS OVER and she was going to end up at Lucas's, like she'd told herself she was wasn't going to do. She had the whole drive home to congratulate herself for going out with a friend and reclaiming some of the social life she'd given up after graduation.

She shoved the shifter into drive. *Thunk.*

The idle speed increased. She shifted back into park. The motor didn't slow down.

"Fuck." She shifted back to drive. There was no change. The ever-present check-engine light was on.

She pressed on the gas but went nowhere. Killing the engine, she slammed the steering wheel with her free hand. "Fuck!"

A tap on her window broke into the tantrum she wanted to keep having. Lucas opened the door without being asked. Cool September evening air whirled into her car. She should've worn a sweater.

He'd waited for her before leaving. A small gesture and one he didn't think twice about, but it was one that added to the way he made her feel special without trying. He certainly didn't try. When he did thoughtful things like waiting for her to pull out of the bar before he left, it amplified the confusion inside of her.

"I think it finally died," she said, glaring at the darkened dashboard.

"From you beating it to death?"

She flipped him off and his laugh echoed into the night, prompting her reluctant smile. Her anxiety lessened, but not much. She'd turned down working at the bar this weekend. For once, she'd felt financially secure enough that she didn't have to work every free moment and could spend time with her family and friends. "Is there any chance you have a towrope in your truck?"

"Honey, I'm a country boy. Of course I have a towrope in my truck."

She rolled her eyes, but her smile didn't disappear.

Working together, they towed her car to her house. Sarah's shadow hovered behind the living room curtain. Nothing got past the woman. Any sound outside of the routine and she was on it. Lucas's pickup pulling in with Trina steering her car behind him was definitely outside of the routine.

Lucas maneuvered her as close to the garage as possible but out of the way of the other vehicles.

Sarah was outside before the engines were killed. Her fluffy royal-blue robe was slung around her and she'd shoved her bare feet into her cowboy boots. "It finally bit the dust, huh?" Her brow was creased as she frowned at the car.

Trina nodded and let Lucas unhook the towrope while she talked to Sarah. From her look of concern, Sarah was wondering the same thing she was. How would she get to school and back? To work? Mom was going out of town on Sunday for a week-long conference and Sarah needed her pickup for the ranch. They didn't keep beaters around to waste money on insurance and registration.

She was left without wheels, living out of town. A taxi would waste money and there was no such thing as Uber in Moore.

Sarah looked her over. "But you're all right?"

"Yeah. I didn't even get out of my parking spot."

"There's that at least. We'll worry about the rest in the morning. You coming inside or..." Sarah jerked her head toward Lucas's land.

"I want to talk to Lucas first." She wasn't ready to admit that yeah, she was heading next door to get laid. If she never reached that level of comfort with her parents, that was just fine with her.

Lucas stashed the rope in his pickup and gestured inside. "Wanna ride?"

"It's so far. I don't know how I'll ever repay you," she joked.

"We'll figure out something." He didn't have to go more than ten miles an hour to circle out of her yard and down to the entrance of his.

Passing by the garage that housed the Chevy gave her an idea. "You got that running, right?"

His expression didn't change. "I've been trying to sell it. Someone's coming to look at it Sunday."

"Think you can put it off until I get the car fixed?" *Or drain my savings to buy a new one?*

He stopped in his usual spot outside the house. "I really need to sell it, Trina."

"I know. I'll treat it well, but I can't miss class. And I can't even risk being late for work. Marilyn might've hired me because of you, but that doesn't mean she'll back off her standards." She waited for him to relent. He knew what Marilyn was like. One minute late and the poor soul was in her office and shaking.

If Trina lost that job, she could kiss getting into nursing school goodbye. No one who'd been fired had gotten into the nursing program. Trina knew of three people, but their stories were legendary and they weren't nurses.

"Trina…"

"Lucas, I just paid for a semester and have barely started saving for next semester. Brayden had a growth spurt after I bought new clothes for the school year. I could really use the help. I promise I won't damage the pickup."

His expression was tortured, and not because he was worried about her and how she'd get through the financial roadblocks dropped on her road of life. She knew him well enough to know that he regretted letting her down, but he wasn't relenting. What was so special about the pickup that he couldn't loan it out? And why wasn't he telling her?

"Fine. I'll figure it out myself like usual." She wrenched on the door handle and spilled out. Before slamming the door, she turned back. His face was a mask of regret and remorse. "We used to be friends. Then you quit talking to me. I thought we were at least friends again, but I can see clearly what my purpose is."

The bang of the door rang like gunshot through the empty night.

She stormed toward her place, hoping she didn't twist an ankle being careless in the dark.

"Trina! It's not like that."

She spun around. "I don't see how it's not." Shoving a hand through her hair, she scanned the dark yard. Crickets continued to chirp like there weren't two humans having an argument right on top of them. He had a reason for not helping her and he wasn't going to tell her what it was. That burned. She thought she'd meant more to him than sex. "Okay, I'm sorry. It's not just the pickup. It's *us*. We haven't gone on one date."

"We have—"

"We pretended to. Once. And don't you dare count the wedding where your cousin called me by your ex-wife's name. I come over here. We fuck. I leave."

"I thought you were worried about what Brayden would think."

She planted her hands on her hips. "What is there to tell him? Here's Lucas, the guy that's never seen in public with me. Between you and Pax, I have a lot of work to do to keep him from treating his future dates like an afterthought."

Lucas winced. Small satisfaction. She hadn't even brought

up how he'd hurt her when he'd stood her up because Shaylee had once again stormed into his life like a cyclone that sucked all the life out of him.

"So excuse me. I have to go figure out how I'm going to get to work and school, or if I have to go back to working at the bar while someone else helps Brayden with his homework and reads him bedtime stories." Her boots scraped against the grass as she turned.

He said her name, but she walked faster.

Close. So close. She'd almost let him in, but life had taught her long ago not to trust a man in her life.

CHAPTER 12

$\mathcal{L}$ucas shook hands with the guy who'd just bought his pickup. Leave it to fate to stomp on him and actually sell the pickup less than forty-eight hours after Trina had accused him of using her for sex.

He hadn't been.

He liked being with her—clothes on or off.

Yet he could see how she'd think that. His pride urged him to stay silent, but now that he held a money order in his hand that'd tide him over until his fall contract was paid, he owed her an explanation.

The pickup he'd put countless hours into drove off and he was left alone, like he'd been all weekend.

A million reasons why he shouldn't go over to her place ran through his head. What if Davina or Sarah ran him off? What if she refused to talk to him? What if she was gone for the day?

None of it stopped him. The hurt that had been scrawled over her face propelled him forward until he was on her doorstep, knocking.

Movement to the left caught his eye. Brayden disappeared

behind the barn. That giant rock pile was still back there. Lucas and Trina used to play on it for hours until one of their parents tracked them down.

Those were the days. He and Trina running all over the land. Hiding from chores. Making a fort in an old shed that used to be on his land. They'd had fun all day long.

That was what he'd reverted to doing with her—but only in a very adult and extremely satisfying way.

It wasn't the same for her, though.

Trina opened the door, hand on her hip, frown on her face. She didn't say a word.

"Can we talk?"

She had to consider it. Damn. He'd known this was a potential outcome, and he'd have to suck it up, but—

The screen clicked open and she stepped back. "Mom's gone for the week and Sarah's getting groceries."

"Brayden's heading to the rock pile."

She didn't smile, but her heavy expression lightened. "He found a garter snake last week and thinks he can catch one."

"We used to do that. Remember?"

"I remember a lot of stuff we used to do together," she said flatly.

He followed her into the living room. She sank into the recliner by the couch. Did she remember the last time they'd been on this couch together? Probably, or she wouldn't have chosen a seat somewhere else.

Jumping right in, he got to the point. "I needed the money from the pickup sale to pay for Dad's care. The farm is in trouble."

Trina's brows popped up. "How much in trouble?"

"Let me clarify." Lucas wiped his hands over his face and rested his elbows on his knees. He stared at the floor as he spoke. "The farm is doing okay. I mean I've had some issues that didn't help, but I'm insured. Paying for Dad's care on top of the farm doesn't leave me much of a living wage."

Understanding dawned in her eyes. "I can't imagine how hard it is to cover the cost of the nursing home."

"It's not just that. The divorce cleaned me out. Half of everything went to her." He spread his hands when her gaze turned defensive—for him. "She was my wife."

"But the farm paid for her school and vacations."

He'd been through all this and honestly, he didn't have the energy to make the journey again. "Her paycheck also went into the farm or into Dad's care." He anticipated the next argument. "Yes, it was a family farm going back to my great-grandparents. All that was hashed out in the divorce. Painfully."

"So it was either pay up or pay more lawyer fees and maybe have to split it all anyway."

Relieved she grasped the situation, he nodded. Rehashing it, even on his behalf, would only unearth all the pain and resentment he'd buried.

"I already took an advance on my contract to pay the nursing home. Until I deliver my corn in November, I won't have another source of income for the nursing home."

"What about direct to market sales?"

"It'll help me cover costs until I deliver on the contract. I got stuck in this rut of taking commodity contracts, but I need to grow the business and sell more than two commodities. But really—I still don't know what I'm doing. Farmers nowadays go to school for this shit. Four years of college *after* growing up in the biz. I just tailed Dad and did what he told me and before I knew it, the whole operation was mine."

She pushed her hand through her hair. The sides had been trimmed so her hair was longer on top, giving her more attitude. "You've farmed for over ten years and you're still in the black. Don't be so hard on yourself."

He uttered what had weighed on his mind for years. "Maybe I wouldn't be in this situation if I was educated."

"Why did you plant what you did this year?"

He thought back to the notes scrawled on his desk with market prices, contract rates, and what he'd estimated he could fulfill.

Before he could answer, she asked another question. "Have you ever taken a loss?"

Had he expected sympathy? He didn't get it. "I mean with insurance—"

"I hear a no." Trina sat forward. "You know what you're doing. You have a major expense that not many people have to plan for in circumstances that not many people have to deal with. Your dad's health. Your mom's death. Your extended family and the divorce."

When she put it like that. He wasn't even in his mid thirties and it had all happened in less than a lifetime. "I wish I could take you out. Have more nights like at Tyler's, but without the drunk confrontation."

"We can still go out. I know how to have fun on a budget. And I can even treat once in a while." She gave him a pointed look. "Without throwing it in your face."

No one treated him but Aunt Marilyn. But Trina wasn't without her own hardships. "What are you doing about the car?"

"Right now, it's either three thousand for a transmission or a two-thousand-dollar beater than smells like mothballs. We're still looking for another car that hasn't sat dead in a field for a while."

"I'll ask around and find you a better option."

"You don't have to—"

"I'm not doing it because I have to." He crouched in front of her. "I want to." He should've thought about it before.

"Thank you."

Running his hands along her thighs, he leaned in. Two days without touching her was like forever. "And I'm picking you up in the morning."

"Sarah said she can give me a ride after Brayden catches the bus. You need to get out into the field."

He chuckled. "So does Sarah." He touched his forehead to hers. "Let me help."

The front door banged open. Lucas tensed to scramble to the couch, but Trina gripped his arms.

Brayden skidded to a stop when he hit the living room. "Are you two dating?" He sounded horrified at seeing his mom with a guy, yet curious.

Trina glanced at him like she was seeking his approval.

Lucas answered. "If she lets me. Think I can steal her away this weekend for a night out?"

Brayden shrugged. "I don't care. Mom, can I have a snack?"

"Yes, but wash your hands first."

Lucas was still close to Trina, not far from being able to kiss her, yet he was a front row witness to the mom-son interaction that he'd previously been excluded from. He didn't want to fuck this up. She was taking more than a chance on him. She was relying on him to help her. Few people were given that opportunity after too many had failed her.

Brayden dove into the kitchen, calling, "What's for supper?"

"Spaghetti!" A hint of exasperation rang in her voice. "He's already asked twice."

With Brayden in another room, Lucas finally did what he'd been aching to do since Friday. Pressing his lips to hers, he kept the kiss PG-13. No tongue—maybe a little tongue—and no other touching besides where his hands rested on her thighs. A cupboard door banged and he broke apart.

Trina kept her voice low. "Can I come over tonight?"

~

LAUGHTER FILLED the house when Trina walked in. Lucas was at the table, cards fanned in his hands. Brayden was across from him and Sarah sat to the side.

What the hell? Sarah hated playing cards. But then, Brayden had his nana wrapped around his finger.

"Whatcha playing?" she asked.

"Rummy?" Lucas frowned at his cards. "Or Go Fish, I can't tell. But Sarah and I are losing."

Trina grinned. Her shift at the center was done, but she had to turn and burn to work a few hours at the bar for Loel. The date she and Lucas had made, and gotten Brayden's blessing for, was tomorrow night. She could've picked up a shift then. But a real date. Her first one ever. And with the neighbor she'd written off years ago. And again last week. But he was back and, she hoped, here to stay.

Her new old car was in the driveway. Lucas had been right. He'd found her a well-used but well-cared-for car. He'd had his friends Jesse and Brock check it over before she'd bought it, supplying her with a list of problems along with their assurances that the car was mechanically sound for several thousand miles yet. And that they'd take care of any issues that sprang up.

Her chest swelled when she thought of how much they'd helped her. She'd served both of them in the bar over the years and was friendly enough but not close. And Jesse, well, he'd gone from infamous to hero.

How long had she lived in the community and not really felt like a part of it? Lucas and his family had been her community, but when Herman had started getting sick, she'd lost them. Otherwise, her moms weren't easy to get to know. Easier to avoid insults that way and dodge being the talk of the town—and they'd been quite the talk in their day.

Trina shrugged out of her sweater. She needed to dig out a heavier coat. These scrubs were like walking naked outside. They did nothing to block the wind and had no insulating power whatsoever. "I'm going to grab a bite to eat and head to the bar."

"There's a plate for you in the fridge," Sarah said as she laid a card on the table.

Trina rivaled Superman in the speed of her outfit change. Dressed in jeans and a long-sleeved gray shirt, she ate at the table with her card players.

"Your mom will be home soon," Sarah said, tossing down the card in her hand. "I give up."

Trina smiled at the triumphant look on Brayden's little face. It must be one of his made-up games that no one but him could win.

"I have to run to town for a few groceries." Lucas popped up and went to the cupboard. He filled a glass with water and set it by her. She could so get used to this. "Mind if I stop in?"

"Not at all." When they'd first started sleeping together, they'd only seen each other a few times a week. Flash forward, and every day they made an excuse to connect. Like when they'd been younger. Either she ran over there, or he showed up on her doorstep.

Leaving was bittersweet. She didn't want to, but leaving Brayden in capable hands did more for her stress and stamina to keep up these hours studying and working than anything else. Throw in Lucas, and she wished she could stay in for the night. It would be one of the best Friday nights she'd had in a long time. Another time. Lucas wasn't going anywhere.

The hour passed. She filled drinks and took appetizer

orders. There was no band tonight, no DJ, just the country selections the customers chose from the modern jukebox.

Warm tingles spread across her shoulders. She looked toward the door. Lucas was here. His gaze was on her as he wove through the tables. He hadn't changed out of the Levi's and brown *Moore Implements* sweatshirt he'd worn earlier, but it didn't matter. The brim of his cap shaded his eyes, amplifying the dark promise in them. His swagger was the same, but it screamed intent. Like he knew she'd go over to his place after work even though they had a date for tomorrow.

She met him halfway to the bar.

"I'll sit at the table in the corner since it's not that busy." He dipped his head to murmur, "Or I'd be tempted to distract you behind the bar."

"You're always tempted."

His deep laugh trailed behind her as he settled into his seat. She grabbed his usual drink and knowing he'd only have the one, she snagged a glass of water.

She filled a drink order for a table in the same area and arranged them on her tray. Feminine laughter caught her attention. Piling through the door were four women, and one caught her eye immediately.

Shaylee.

She was smiling with the rest of her party and Trina's heart sank when they headed to the same section of the bar Lucas sat alone in. Hadn't he been hurt enough?

Aaaand they took a table in her area. She'd have to take their order when she delivered Lucas's drinks.

Hefting her tray, she stopped by Lucas's table first. He was playing some sort of farming game on his phone. "Can't get enough?"

"I make more money in the game." His smile vanished when Shaylee flipped her hair as she was taking a seat. Trina tried not to witness the tense moment as his ex gave him a small wave, acting as if Trina were invisible. She was just the pesky neighbor girl in Shaylee's estimation.

Lucas nodded and slid his gaze up to hers.

"Sorry," Trina said and set the drink down. "I brought your beer first so I could give you a warning."

He wrapped his hand around the cold bottle. "It's a small town. It happens."

"If I weren't working, we could put on another show like at the wedding."

A smile lifted his lips. Nice and even. He wasn't feeling the humor. "Except with her baby bump, no one will mistake you two."

Yeah. The baby bump. Shaylee's trendy patterned top smoothed over her belly, as tight as her leggings. With her knee-high boots, she looked as sophisticated as always. Trina had never had a problem wondering how Lucas could fall for someone like her. Most guys did.

"I've gotta wait on them too." Trina didn't want to leave, but she had three more hours left on her shift.

"I hope they leave you a good tip."

They wouldn't, but Trina wasn't worried about the tip money tonight.

She was as courteous as she needed to be to the group of women. Shaylee treated her like she always had, like the help. An hour ticked by. Lucas finished his drink and came to the bar.

"I'll take another beer," he said, setting his cash on the counter. "I won't be able to watch you work as a nurse, so I need to live it up now."

"You might get in a little trouble hanging out at the center."

"Is that where you want to work when you're done?"

She got his beer from the cooler and slid it across to him.

"I really enjoy it. Marilyn's tough but fair, so yeah. If I get into nursing school and graduate, I hope to stay there."

A customer called her name.

Lucas returned to his table as more customers spilled into the bar. She was so caught up in taking orders and cleaning tables that she didn't pay attention to him. Sneaking a peek to get her through the rest of the shift, she stumbled. Shaylee was across from Lucas, sipping the motherfucking water she'd brought for him.

A woman at the table she was by reached her arm out, like she was ready to catch her. "Are you okay?"

Trina didn't register who, only muttered. "Yeah, thanks."

Her thoughts churned over Lucas. How was he doing? What did Shaylee want? What were they talking about?

She refused to be reduced to a jealous, needy girlfriend.

The next hour crawled by. The women Shaylee had come with left. And Shaylee stayed with Lucas.

She was my wife.

That statement shouldn't make her so defensive, but it was Lucas's relationship with Shaylee summed up so simply.

Nathan Hart was her dad, but that didn't give him allowance to treat her like shit. She'd cut her own dad out of her life, but Lucas couldn't shake a toxic ex.

He didn't realize how toxic she was, that was the problem.

But he would, right? His face was somber and his trademark smile was absent. He would come to his own conclusion. She had to believe he would.

The next hour crawled by. Shaylee stayed at Lucas's table and drank all that damn water. Trina didn't bother to go back and check on drinks.

The rest of her shift, she was an efficient robot. Take orders, clear tables, wipe counters, and serve food. The kitchen shut down, and she was done.

She didn't care how long Lucas and his ex were going to

stay tucked into the corner all cozy. His demeanor hadn't changed, and no laughter filtered from them. Whatever they talked about, it was heavy.

Well…she was his wife.

Trina finished her tasks and checked out with the manager, wishing she'd never picked up this shift in the first place. She was about to disappear into the back room when Lucas called her name.

Relief poured into her. For once he hadn't forgotten about her thanks to the other woman in his life.

Facing him, her stomach dropped. From the look on his face, he had something to say that she wouldn't like.

"Shaylee needs a ride, then I'll be right home."

What the fuck? "She needs a ride?"

His jaw tightened. "I guess she told her friends she'd catch a ride with me before checking."

Call a taxi. Or her fiancé. "Oh."

"Meet you at my place?"

She nodded like she'd pushed the autopilot button. Lucas turned to leave. Shaylee was strutting out, her blond high-lighted hair arranged over one shoulder. She didn't even look Trina's way.

He followed the woman, but at least he didn't rush. That was something, right?

Trina balled up her apron, grabbed her purse, and didn't bother putting on her jacket before she charged out the back door. She couldn't help but search the lot for his truck. It was easy enough to find. The crowd from the bar had lightened this late.

Lucas climbed into the driver's seat and Shaylee daintily scaled the height into the passenger seat like she was climbing Mount Everest with heeled boots.

He didn't open the door for her. That was something, right?

~

"I JUST CAN'T BELIEVE that he'd make that kind of decision and not consult me." Shaylee rested her head in her hand. She sniffled while her thumb spun her flashy engagement ring in a circle.

"It's crazy," he said as noncommittally as he could.

He was idling in his truck outside of her fiancé's house. They'd been sitting here for over ten minutes. Was Trina at his place yet? Had she lingered at work before leaving? He hoped so. He didn't want to keep her waiting.

The dentist's place was dark. Apparently he was out of town, scoping out jobs in Chicago. And it had been news to Shaylee.

When she'd plunked herself down at the table, he couldn't have been more shocked. It was admittedly hard to linger in the bar with her there and not feel like the loser ex-husband around her circle of friends. *There's the guy Shaylee ran from, drowning his sorrows alone over a beer while playing the farming game his friend's cousin developed. Maybe if he was smart enough, he could've designed his own app.*

He couldn't really parade around declaring Trina was his girlfriend and how he'd given her more orgasms than he could count. It wasn't anyone's business, not even the friends Shaylee had said she discussed their "problematic" sex life with.

If she weren't pregnant, he'd flip the handle and dump her on the sidewalk. "Well, good night."

She looked at him, tears sparkling in her eyes. Her crying. It softened him every time, but this time was different. The tears weren't because of him. "Do you remember how we used to sit outside my parents' house like this when we first started dating?"

He cut his gaze away. They used to make out while sitting in his pickup. "It was a long time ago."

"Yeah," she said sadly. "Those days were so much easier." She gave up spinning her ring like a Wheel of Fortune contestant and laid her hand on his arm.

He bit down on his tongue to keep from jerking. What was she doing?

"Are you doing okay?" Sincerity clogged her tone. "After the last time we talked…"

"I'm fine. My days are still farming and visiting Dad." He couldn't draw away. There was nowhere to go in the cab that wasn't closer to her. The touch was wrong. If she'd touched him like this three years ago, maybe he wouldn't have had a panic attack the first time he'd slept with another woman.

The same woman who might be at his house waiting for him.

"How's he doing?" Shaylee asked.

"Forgetful." Way worse than when she'd left. Deteriorating every year.

"I bet it's hard."

"Look, Shaylee—"

"Are you seeing anyone?"

He clamped his mouth shut. Where was this conversation going? Where was this whole night going? He was supposed to just come to town, relax, and sort of hang out with Trina before they fell into bed.

But he'd been jettisoned back in time, to his married life when he wasn't sure how he was supposed to answer or what the real question was.

"I really need to get going. Early morning."

Hurt crossed her face. "Right. Harvest." She opened her mouth like she was going to ask how that was going, but that would be too out of character. Harvest had been her breaking point. Long days. Long nights. Repeat. She'd been alone and that was unacceptable. "Thank you for the ride, Lucas. I knew I could count on you."

Since when? Hadn't that been the point of the divorce? He was unreliable as a provider, a disappointment in bed, and an all-around embarrassment. He took his first easy breath as she exited the pickup.

Look at the time. Twenty minutes of waiting for her to get out.

He flew home, kicking up a cloud of dust in his taillights. His heart sank lower as he pulled in and saw Trina waiting on his doorstep, his dogs at her feet. He should've left his house unlocked, but it was habit instilled in him from his city-girl ex-wife. One she'd joked sarcastically about as she turned the deadbolt she'd insisted he install. *I'd hate for someone to steal our dollar-store silverware.*

Just like the last encounter with Shaylee, he was soothed by the sight of Trina. He just wanted her taste and her touch to wash away the layer of the past he was steeped in. He walked away from his encounters with Shaylee feeling like old, sticky flypaper. Covered in dust, grit, and the occasional dead fly. Useful once, but only for a short time.

Trina's even gaze followed him as he parked by her car.

When he got out, he wanted nothing more than to gather her in his arms and dive under the covers. The dogs came over to sniff him. They'd bunk down in the shed where he'd installed a pet door and arranged a corner with beds for each of them.

The air was crisp with the scent of impending rain and those few moments before water hit the ground and cast up its earthy odor. Rain was one of his favorite smells, but he couldn't stop to enjoy it.

He jogged over to her. "Sorry about that."

She curled her arms into herself, burying them in her

sweater as she straightened from the step. "I should've gone home."

"Absolutely not." He passed her without a kiss only to unlock the door. She was chilly and needed to get inside. "After the last hour and a half, there's no one I'd rather be with than you."

"Right. Because you weren't with me for the last hour. And a half."

He glanced over his shoulder. Her tone was not like her, and he was shit at picking up when something was bothering a woman. Her expression didn't give anything away. She wasn't smiling. More like expectant.

"No, and I rather it had been you." He hip-checked the door open and held it wide for her to go inside first. Mr. Whiskers meowed and met them at the door. "The cat already got fed. Don't believe him."

That earned him a little smile. He stepped out of his boots. She didn't take hers off.

Another warning bell went off. "Is everything okay?"

She gazed up at him with the same passive expression. "Should it be?"

"I hope so." What was she talking about? He thought back on the night. She'd been, for lack of a better term, *happy* at the bar. Now she was drawing farther and farther away the longer they talked. "Is this about Shaylee? I swear there's nothing there anymore. She mostly talked about her fiancé's plans to move after they're married and how he went about it without talking to her and how much she'll miss Moore."

"To you?"

"Right? She wanted to keep talking when we got to her place." He shrugged. "Maybe she was lonely because Dr. Do-Me was gone."

"And you're okay with her parking it next to you and going on and on about him?"

"I don't know what to think, but I'm not wishing she'd come running back to me. So it doesn't really matter?" It was weird though. He couldn't deny it. "I'm not a player in her game of life."

Trina muttered, "Are you sure about that?"

He slid his arms under hers and tugged her to him. "Yes. I'm a player in our date tomorrow night."

"Did you tell her you were seeing me?"

"It's none of her business." *Are you seeing anyone?* The question still unsettled him. "She has no say in my life anymore."

She softened ever so slightly in his embrace. "Tonight. Our date is later tonight. I should probably let you get some sleep."

"Rain's on the way. I get to sleep in." Not for long. Aside from being in the combine, there were plenty of other duties to do. Especially in his office, where he was itching to plan his next season and search online for another fixer-upper he could make a few bucks on.

Or maybe he could find a part-time job that would allow him to keep the farm. A side hustle with benefits. It was like finding a unicorn in his haystacks.

"I have to study tomorrow." She didn't move to leave. He took it as a good sign.

"I'll make up being late to you. I promise."

The look she gave him was challenging. "I'd like to see what you do to try."

He grinned. "It starts by taking your shirt off."

CHAPTER 13

"Jt's going to rain." Herman squinted out the window. "I need to get out in the fields." He wore charcoal-gray slippers and his housecoat hung open. He barely stood taller than her anymore. There were no more fields for him, but he was talking. Today was one of his good days.

Trina finished changing the fitted sheet on his bed. "You have time for a bite to eat first, right?"

His rheumy eyes snapped to her.

"It's almost time to eat," she explained. "The food will be here soon."

She didn't say that it was lunchtime or Herman would fret about how he hadn't gotten outside to work yet. Working around patients with dementia was getting easier as she learned to navigate the individual and varying worlds their minds created.

"I'll wait to eat until Barbara gets here."

Trina's chest ached whenever he said that. She finished making the bed. By the time she was done, his food tray was brought in. Herman hardly ate in the main dining area. It upset him too much after all those years of packing lunch in the field or eating alone in the house while Barbara was at work.

After seeing that he was settled and doing well, she buzzed out of the room. It was time for her own lunch. Next to the door to the staff break room, Lucas leaned against the wall with a nylon, navy-blue lunch bag tucked under his arm.

He wore a red ball cap that contrasted with his gray *Moore Mudders* sweater. He stood out in a pool of scrubs' and residents' cotton attire. He wore jeans every day but she never tired of looking at him.

"What are you doing here?" Since she was still on the clock, she stopped short of giving him a kiss.

"I asked Aunt Marilyn when your break was and figured I could see you and come hang with Dad."

The warmth in her belly was becoming more frequent. She'd frozen up after the night she'd been left waiting in the dark for him to finish catering to Shaylee. She could tell he'd been oblivious to her hurt, but she believed that he didn't wish to get back together with his ex.

And that wasn't the reason the night had upset her.

Okay, maybe a little. She was only human.

It was that she'd been left hanging again while he catered to Shaylee or the aftereffects of Shaylee.

He hadn't told his ex about them. No, it wasn't Shaylee's business, and yes, it was selfish of Trina to want to establish her status with Lucas, but he was right. It was between them. The town was small and Shaylee would find out soon enough.

His phone buzzed in his pocket. She lifted a brow.

"Whoever it is can call back later." He flourished the lunch bag. "I have sandwiches."

She put her hand on her heart and mock gasped. "With chips?"

"Cheetos. Only the best for you, babe."

She waved her badge over the electronic lock to let him into the empty break room. While she clocked out, he picked a table and started unpacking his stash. Sandwiches wrapped in baggies, small orange bags of chips, and juice boxes.

Her laughter bubbled out of her. "Is that bologna and Cheetos like your mom used to pack us when we were kids?"

"I learned from the best." He produced two cans of sparkling water. "Those juice boxes are too small."

Her stomach growled and they each dug in. He'd even used plain white bread, not the healthy nut stuff they'd hated as kids—and was all she bought now.

Shaking her bag of chips to make sure she'd nabbed all the crumbs, she finished chewing. "Remember that little shed we made a fort in?" The tiny shack had probably been a chicken coop or something before she or Lucas had been born. It had technically been on his property, but it had bordered their land, and they'd stored all their cool finds in it. Big sticks. Rocks. Their own toys they'd brought from home.

He nodded. "The one in the back quarter. Mom had a heart attack when she found out." He mimicked his mom. "'Good God, you kids are going to get hantavirus in there.'"

"I can't believe we didn't get sick with something."

"Maybe it was all the running around in the dirt that kept us healthy."

She balled up her wrappers to throw away. "I'm sure the stock pond was perfectly sanitary with all that manure runoff. While destroying that shed broke my heart as a kid, I'm grateful your dad let us clear our treasure out of there and help with the process."

"He bribed us with s'mores over the bonfire of the rubble."

She grinned at the image of her and Lucas licking their goopy fingers at the edge of the fire pit. "As a parent, I approve of the way he handled it. He could've torn it down without telling us." She sighed wistfully and lobbed her trash toward the garbage bin. It sailed inside. "I miss it though. At least the rock pile is still there."

"It was fun. Our own little fort. Kept us out of trouble."

"Until you started dating and had no time for your tomboy friend."

He scowled as he gathered his own lunch remains. "It wasn't like that."

It was, but she didn't argue. The shed. The rock pile. Riding horse together. Those were memories she'd buried because they'd hurt too badly once he quit talking to her. Just because he didn't realize how he'd vacated her life, creating a vacuum with no other friends, didn't make the memories bitter. Now that he was here, those moments came back and made her smile.

She glanced at the time. The half hour had gone by way too quickly. "I came from your dad's room before I got here."

"How's he doing?"

"He's in the past. Worried about harvest."

Lucas's smile was sad. "Once a farmer…" He zipped his bag and helped her clean the table. "I was thinking that we should take Brayden for a ride."

"Has he been pestering you too?"

A beat of confusion passed over his face. "He hasn't mentioned a thing."

"Oh, well he's been asking to go for a ride before winter comes. And I really should take him before I'm stuck studying for finals."

"Do you work next weekend?"

She nodded. "Only Saturday."

"It's a date."

There went the warmth spreading through her. She loved when he said that. "And Mom asked if you want to come for supper tonight. She's making homemade pizza."

He rubbed his chin. "Hmm. More bologna sandwiches or your mom's pizza with the dough she makes from scratch."

She bit the inside of her cheek. "I'll tell her you couldn't pass up the white bread in your house."

"Don't you dare. What time should I be there?"

"I get off at three thirty, but I need to study. She's planning six thirty."

"See you then. We can even take the horses out after. It'll be a nice October evening." He drifted closer, looking toward the door as he dipped his head for a kiss.

Their lips had barely touched when the handle on the door clicked. She stepped back and he straightened before the door swung open.

One of the middle-aged cooks entered, her eyes widening in surprise. "Oh, Lucas. I'm not used to seeing you in here."

"Well, I'm going to Dad's and making sure he gets a belly full of your mashed potatoes."

The cook chuckled. "Baked potatoes today, but I thought of Herman and how he loves his mashed potatoes with butter on top." She bustled to the fridge.

In the hallway, Lucas murmured in her ear, "There'll be more of that kissing tonight."

Her face burned hot. Only she heard his words, but the nursing home was its own ecosystem of small talk, and word was spreading that she was seeing Herman's son.

"I'm counting on it," she whispered as she sauntered away. His groan resonated behind her.

~

Putting his tools away in the shop, Lucas checked the time. Just enough to run through the shower, wash the grease off, and get over to Trina's for supper.

He hadn't had Davina's homemade pizza for fifteen years. Which meant she'd had that many years to perfect her technique. His mouth watered as he jogged inside.

Mr. Whiskers greeted him before beelining to his bowl. Lucas filled his dish and dove into the shower.

He passed over clean clothes, dressing in cleanish jeans and the sweater he'd worn before working in the shop all afternoon. He was presentable enough for dinner, and if they went riding, it wouldn't matter if he got these clothes smelling like horse sweat.

Just in time. He grabbed his phone and banged out of the house. His foot crunched in the gravel when his phone rang. Was Trina worried he was late?

He answered without looking, pouring all of his intentions for her tonight into his greeting. "Hey."

"Hi." Shaylee. She sounded relieved. "I wasn't sure you'd answer."

Damn. He wouldn't have if he'd seen it was her. She'd held him up a few too many times. "Is something wrong?"

"Remember my cousin Riley?"

Riley… Riley… "No, sorry."

"She was younger than us, actually my cousin Terry's girl?"

He recalled a little blond girl with two missing front teeth. He hadn't seen her since Shaylee's family reunion in high school. "Oh, okay. Yeah, I remember her. They live in North Carolina, right?"

"She was killed in a car accident last night."

Air punched out of his lungs. "I'm sorry." He slowed his

walk toward Trina's place. "You doing okay?" He'd ask how Terry was, but, yeah. How else would he be doing?

Her sigh gusted over the phone. "I am. I can't go there and Terry and I aren't super close, but it's hard, you know? I just saw them last year."

"Well, thanks for letting me know."

"I think it hit me harder now that I'm going to be a mom."

Dropping his head back to stare at the clouds pillowed in the sky, he cursed his luck. He was going to be late. Kicking Shaylee off the phone while she was reeling from a death in her family was too callous for him.

He paused in the line of trees. It was chillier in the shade, but he could lean against a scraggly tree.

"Everything will be fine, Shaylee." He didn't have the power to promise that, but she needed to hear it.

"I feel like…" She sniffled. "I mean, my mom called and I needed to talk to someone and… Drake is at a conference."

Her dentist was gone again. Did he know Shaylee called him? What would he think if he did? Lucas had too many problems, and a jealous fiancé shouldn't be one of them.

Her mom would be better for her to talk to. "Maybe you should call—"

"I can't fly there either. I'm not due until the beginning of the year, but I hate flying alone, you know that."

"Then take Drake with you."

"He can't get out of work."

"Won't your parents be going?" This was a variation on many conversations they'd had during their time together. She'd panic over decisions big and small and he'd offer solutions until she got angry with him. *Can't you offer support for once?*

That statement he'd been free to take many ways.

"They hopped in the car to head to North Carolina as

soon as they got the call. I don't know, Lucas. How am I going to do this?"

He didn't need to ask what she was asking about. Motherhood. Life with the dentist that wasn't as idyllic as she'd imagined. "You'll be fine. You always are."

As she continued about the guilt she felt over missing the funeral and her own worries about the baby, he gazed at Trina's house. If Trina were in Shaylee's situation, she would have the same concerns. But she'd power forward. Afraid of flying or not, she'd get her ass to the funeral, and if she couldn't, then she'd send a card and offer what support she could from Moore, Minnesota.

Being alone didn't stop Trina.

"Like I said," he reiterated after she paused. "You'll be fine. Listen, I've gotta go."

"Oh, yeah. Okay. Um, thank you, Lucas. I mean it."

"No problem. Take care, and do you mind sending me Terry's address so I can send a card?"

"You're always so thoughtful."

He almost pulled the phone from his ear to stare at it. Was this the same Shaylee who'd accused him of being insensitive to her needs?

Hanging up, he tucked the phone into his pocket and trotted across the yard, up Trina's stairs, and knocked.

She opened the door, her expression playful. "Mom insisted on waiting for you. *I* was willing to start without you."

That was the difference between Shaylee and Trina. Shaylee would've waited and used his tardiness as a reason to stretch him through the wringer. Trina wouldn't have let it stop her. She wouldn't have let *him* stop her.

If he weren't careful, she'd be so far ahead he wouldn't catch up.

The thought sobered him. "Thanks for waiting. Sorry for

the…" Admitting his ex had interfered in their plans again didn't seem like the best idea right now.

"I saw you lurking in the trees. Must've been an important phone call." She twined her fingers through his to lead him toward the kitchen.

"It was one I couldn't get away from," he muttered. She looked at him over her shoulder, an unreadable expression on her face. Her grip loosened, but he tightened his. "Seriously. Thanks for waiting."

"I wasn't going to wait forever."

"I know. And I'm glad. But I'm grateful today since it's your mom's pizza."

Brayden slid into the kitchen as they gathered around the table. Lucas took the extra chair by Trina that was set out just for him.

Davina dished out the cheesiest pizza he'd ever seen.

"Good thing we planned our horse outing tonight," Trina said. "Brayden wanted to stay at his dad's next weekend."

Brayden grinned and dug into his slice.

"No problem." As he ate, he and Sarah went back and forth about getting the rest of his crops in.

Brayden leaned over the table to grab a second slice. "Hey, Lucas. Want to stay and watch the new Star Wars movie?"

Trina put her hand on her son's arm and gently said, "Next time, ask if someone can pass the pizza."

"I could reach it."

Lucas chuckled. "If it's okay with the ladies, I'd love to stay. I won't even spoil it for you."

Brayden blinked and paused with his slice halfway to his mouth. "You've already seen it?"

He'd had too much time in the last two years to watch all kinds of TV. "Maybe not the newest one."

Before he dug back into his food, he caught the slight smile on Trina's face.

This is what I want for the rest of my life. This.

His phone vibrated against his ass cheek, but it'd be rude to check it in the middle of dinner. And it was probably just Shaylee again. He'd check it the next time he went to the bathroom.

CHAPTER 14

*E*ver so slowly, Trina drained the bedpan into the toilet. She'd learned early—dumping it caused splash back. Slow and steady won the urine game. The more she worked at the center, the less she picked up shifts at the bar.

Lucas had something to do with that too. Between studying and spending time with him and her family, she declined shifts at Barley 'n' Hops more often. Her old manager had called her for tonight, but she was in the middle of her Saturday shift at the nursing home.

She'd finished up in the resident's room and was walking down the hall, still rubbing sanitizer on her hands, when she spotted her supervisor.

"Oh, there you are, Trina. You can go ahead and take your break now. I was just in the break room and your purse is dancing a jig in your locker."

A stab of alarm pierced her chest. Mom and Sarah rarely called, only leaving messages. She zipped to the break room and went straight for the wall of lockers on one side. In record time, she spun the dial on the lock until it clicked open.

Digging her phone out, she groaned at the message waiting for her. "Shit." Three missed calls from Pax.

Hitting his number, she counted to ten.

He answered on eight. "Trina…about tomorrow…"

"Pax, you *cannot* cancel on him again." The disappointment she'd felt every time her dad had bailed on her welled up. Why promise in the first place if he'd never planned on coming to town?

"You know I don't like to do it either." No, she didn't. "He begged and I said yes before asking Emily what we had planned."

"So you waited all week before checking with her? He's been excited to see you."

"We have company coming—"

"And God forbid they meet your son." She clenched her jaw.

"Trina, don't be difficult."

The first date with Pax she could understand. Maybe the second. But how lonely had she been when she'd said yes to dates three and four? Pax was a noodle. Give him a little stress and he bent and slid off the spoon.

"Fine." Begging him wouldn't change his mind. He was rock-solid on his determination to bail on his word. "But I'm not being the bad guy. You tell him."

"But he doesn't have a phone—"

"Call Mom or Sarah." She hung up. Her heart raced and she was breathing hard. Fucking Pax.

She hit Lucas's number.

The drone of the combine didn't drown out his greeting.

"Is there any chance you can still ride horse tomorrow with me and Brayden?"

He didn't miss a beat. "Pax bailed."

"He bails more than any rancher in the county. But if you have to be in the field, it's okay." She shouldn't have asked as soon as she heard what he was doing.

"I'll make it work. Don't worry."

"Thanks, Lucas."

"Whatcha wearing?"

She groaned. "I swear you only think about one thing."

"About you? Yes. For the whole day in this beast? Also, yes." His laughter over the line rippled right through her belly. Her shift was early and she'd missed being with him last night. "What time tomorrow?"

"Should we do late afternoon so we can ride and then go grab something to eat? I'll have Brayden help me saddle our horses."

"And I'll ride Gun-Shy over at three."

"See you then."

She hung up, a smile on her face. Tucking her phone away and closing her locker, she kept the stupid grin in place. That man made her insides tumble. If she could've withstood him before, him rearranging his day during his busiest season would have tumbled her walls down completely.

Turning around, she yelped. "Marilyn. Sorry. I was just heading back to work."

"Is your break over?" Marilyn sat at one table and pulled out a chair next to her like she knew Trina had half her time left.

Trina shook her head. "I have a few more minutes."

"Mind if we have a chat?"

All of her earlier glow vacated, leaving a cold spot in her gut. Had she messed up? Had her coworkers complained? A resident? She sat in the chair, more nervous than in her initial interview.

Marilyn crossed one leg over the other. "The deadline for

the LPN program application is in early February but opens November first. Are you applying?"

Her dread didn't disappear. What if Marilyn wanted to tell her not to bother?

"Yes, I plan to apply. The semester will be over in December and I thought I'd wait until then before finishing my application. That way I'll have my grades." Marilyn would know that. Trina was in danger of rambling. Folding her hands together, she willed herself to sit still and not jiggle a foot or twist her fingers together.

Marilyn nodded, her shrewd gaze boring into her. "That's a good idea. I was hoping that you were going to apply to be in the next class. You're doing really well. I know it's not time for your six-month eval yet, but I've been getting really good feedback from your shift supervisors and even from the department manager."

Shock swirled with relief inside her. Marilyn thought she was doing well? She'd been prepared to work here for years and bust her ass before receiving Marilyn's praise. The woman was a notoriously critical boss, but not an unfair one. She just wasn't loose with her compliments.

"You look surprised." The corner of Marilyn's mouth kicked up.

She mulled over what to say next. Honesty was always her best policy, but she didn't want to insult Marilyn. "I'm confident in my work even though this is a brand-new field for me. But I'm aware you have high standards. The praise coming from you, this early, took me off guard."

"Are you worried that it's because you're dating my nephew? That it's the only reason why I think you're doing well?"

Wasn't that how she'd gotten the job? "You weren't going to hire me otherwise." There. It was out there. Trina had needed every opportunity, and maybe being linked to Lucas had opened the door, but earning the rest on her own merit was critical.

Marilyn studied her. Seconds ticked by. It was growing harder and harder not to fidget. Her break was probably over and excuses for why she was late formed in her head. Talking to Marilyn was the best excuse, but she wasn't used to needing one.

"Lucas and I are close, but you know that. After Herman got sick and Barbara died, I saw him as more of a son. I tend to get really protective of the people in my inner circle, and when they don't listen to my advice, I take it personally." Marilyn looked away, regret washing over her face. "Just like when your mom didn't listen to me. We used to be friends, you know."

If she hadn't been shocked before, she was now. Friends? Mom never mentioned Marilyn, not even with a tone of disgust. They must have had a falling-out long before Trina was born.

"We'd been best friends since kindergarten." Marilyn wasn't done pulling the rug out from under her. The woman speared her with that direct, soul-reading gaze. "When she met your father, I warned her against seeing him."

Trina's eyes flew wide. Stomach acid churned until she was afraid she would gag. Having her father dropped in the middle of this type of conversation was like taking a hit to the head. She'd spent years trying not to think about him, and while she might not have succeeded, at least no one else talked about him.

Marilyn spoke more freely. She'd said the worst and was trying to explain. "She was determined to make it work. Oh, we argued. We were best friends and I knew… I suspected…" Marilyn's gaze slid away once more. "That she was, um…"

"A lesbian." The word hovered between them. How would Marilyn react? Trina might've pretended to date Lucas to get the job, but she couldn't stay working for Marilyn if the director had a problem with her moms. But from what Marilyn was saying, the issue was a whole history Trina hadn't been clued in to.

Marilyn's mouth tightened. "I understood why she was determined to make a relationship with him work and not live openly in a small town, but I saw how he was. The way he treated her."

"He wasn't husband of the year." Or dad of the year.

"Does she think— Never mind. That's between me and her, and one of these days I may get over my hurt pride from thirty years ago and try to mend fences. And"— Marilyn straightened, tugging down her suit coat and brushing imaginary dust off the front—"I'll talk to your supervisor and let her know that I detained you during your break."

Trina got up to follow Marilyn out but couldn't keep up. The last part of the conversation had upset the woman.

So Marilyn didn't hate her, but she also didn't deny that Trina was working here because of Lucas. She could live with that.

A few more hours and she was done for the day. Another shift complete at a challenging job that she enjoyed. Brayden was at home with his grandmas. Lucas was stepping in where Pax had failed.

The life she'd worked so hard for was coming to fruition.

Damn phone.

Someone had messaged. Again. Lucas would put twenty dollars down on who it was. Shaylee must be going through an early midlife crisis. What did they call it when they were in their early thirties? Millennial crisis?

It didn't matter. He finished up fixing the bent Haybine jack in his shop so he could get Gun-Shy saddled.

His phone went wild. Oh, hell. She was calling now?

"Yeah," he answered sharply, going for I'm-too-busy-to-talk brusque.

"Lucas. I wasn't sure you would be able to answer. I know how hectic this time of year gets for you."

She knew all right. She'd explained it in painful, detailed, explicit terms when justifying sleeping with her boss.

"What's going on?" He let the lid of his small toolbox slam shut. *See? Busy.*

"Today's the day of the funeral."

He dropped his head, keeping the phone to his ear. It was a hard day for her and those she would normally turn to for support were at the funeral. But what about what's-his-name? "I'm sure it's a hard day for you."

"I wish I could do more, but I'm stuck here."

With no one else to talk to apparently. "Isn't your fiancé around for you?"

"He, um, kinda doesn't want to talk about this anymore." Her voice shook like she was on the verge of tears. Once a douche, always a douche.

"That's too bad, because he's the one you should really be talking to." He tensed. Would that set her off on a tirade about how unreliable he was?

"Right? I've been crying about this all week and today he said he needs a break and left. I guess the golf course is still open." Scorn dripped from her voice.

Until snow fell, the golf course's door was wide open. Or so he'd heard. Usually golfing season was his busy season. But somehow, she'd managed to reach him and not the dentist.

He couldn't stand here talking and risk being late again. Shoving the phone between his ear and shoulder, he wiped his hands off, tossed the rag on the bench, and locked up the shop while she talked.

He crossed his yard to the barn where he kept tack he hadn't used since last year. Gun-Shy didn't get ridden as much as he used to, but maybe with Brayden next door wanting to learn, both Lucas and Gun-Shy would get out more. Have some fun that didn't include beer or a screen.

While he gathered his gear and cramped his neck holding the phone pinched against his shoulder, Shaylee described how each family member was doing, what her mom had said about the cemetery and how serene it was. Lucas kept his movements as quiet as he could. With the nature of the subject, it was just insensitive to be disruptive.

He reached the point where he was going to have to go outside and saddle Gun-Shy. Looking around, he rolled his eyes skyward. What did he think, that he'd find someone who would hang up the phone for him?

Stepping out into the pasture, he scanned the area for his horse. He was about to turn and look around the other side when a nose bumped his shoulder.

Stumbling forward, he threw his hand out and caught the side of the barn. Gun-Shy was waiting patiently behind him. A horse that acted like a lap dog had snuck up on him. Lucas could've gotten a face full of dirt, or worse.

He stroked Gun-Shy's neck. Doing all of this one-handed without hurting himself or his horse wasn't possible. Saddling his horse would have to wait until he got Shaylee off the phone.

Five minutes later, she hit the subject of funeral bouquets —sizes, how many, types of flowers. This was a good time. "I hate to cut this short, but I really have to get back to work." He cringed, that old habit of expecting a tirade about his hours never far away.

"I'm so sorry. I shouldn't have taken up so much of your time."

What was that old movie Dad liked, something about pod people? Had that shit happened in Moore?

With her off the phone he was able to saddle his horse in record time. He swung up and rode over to Trina's place.

It felt good to be out like this again. Gun-Shy's middle was rounder than it used to be, but then again—welcome to the club.

Both Trina and Brayden were atop a horse, both geldings. Sarah held on to the lead rope for Brayden, but Trina was tall and at ease, her hands draped over the saddle horn. Sometimes, he forgot what a country girl she was. When they'd been kids, her long hair had been windblown and tangled half the time. Even then she'd had no time for styling, not when fun was to be had.

He grinned and waved. "Look at you, buddy. You're going to be a pro at this in no time."

Trina sent him a droll look. "He's already asking about steer roping."

His laughter felt good, especially after the heavy subject matter from Shaylee's call. "We picked a perfect afternoon. I don't think it's going to stay this nice in the middle of October for that much longer."

For the next hour and a half, they ambled through the pastures. He and Trina regaled Brayden with all the antics of their younger days. They even stopped at the spot where the shed used to stand.

Disappointment sifted through him as they strolled back into her yard, but the day wasn't over. If they were going out to eat to a sit-down place, he wanted to clean up and change into clothes that didn't smell like he'd bunked down with a horse overnight. Trina said she'd wanted to do the same.

"Give me twenty minutes, and I'll drive over and pick you

two up." He jogged to his house. His phone went off again. Damn.

Before entering, he glanced down. Are you home? Shaylee.

He replied, Only for a little bit longer, and left it at that. She could take the hint.

A quick shower and clothing change later, he was stepping into his boots when an engine sounded outside. Straightening, he peered out the door.

Fuck. No. Shaylee had just pulled into his driveway.

What the hell was she doing here? Panic spread through him like an out-of-control grass fire. His time was ticking down, and he didn't want to make Trina and Brayden wait and wonder. Neither did he want either one to think he was standing them up.

He opened the screen door and stepped out. Shaylee got out of her car with a tearstained face, puffy bags under her eyes, and a bright red nose. He's seen that look a lot in the year before the divorce.

Skipping a greeting, he held open the door. She charged inside without a word, her chin trembling. He stepped in behind her, the door banging shut. How was he going to extract himself from this situation? She was grieving over a loved one's death and had turned to him.

She spun into him, burying her face against his chest. He was torn. What should he do? A man couldn't be in two places at once, and he was already expected somewhere else.

She sniffled between sobs. "I am so sorry, but I didn't know where else to turn. I tried calling Drake, but he's turned off his phone."

Harsh. But at the same time, why the hell hadn't he shut his own phone off? A big part of him hadn't wanted to be a callous bastard. Then again, he would be if he lingered here too much longer. His time was up and two people were waiting on him.

"Shaylee, I gotta…"

Shaylee fisted her hands and his shirt and clung to him as she cried harder.

He patted her on the back. Cradling her in a hug no longer felt right. She was the wrong height. The perfume wasn't right either. And all the hair. But this situation wasn't sexual, only eye opening. She needed comfort, and he didn't think he was the guy to do it.

"Am I a horrible person to live with?" Her voice was muffled against his pec.

Her question startled him. It certainly wasn't one he'd expected when she arrived—or at all.

"I'm not really the one to answer that. You were the one that couldn't live with me anymore."

She tipped her head back, staring at him with blurry red eyes. "I thought so at the time. But looking back, and after living with Drake, I can only remember how good you were to me." She shifted her hands up his shoulders. "You always took such good care of me, and I never appreciated it."

Toward the end of their marriage, Lucas had prayed every night to hear those words from her. Or that she'd decided he really was a good guy and that he hadn't failed her. To heal, he'd taken all the responsibility for the failure. But after Trina? He knew that a marriage took two people, and he couldn't have been the only one that had made mistakes.

Hearing her admit it… He didn't know what to think.

"We were over a long time ago." The day she crawled into bed with another man. Her betrayal had broken him to pieces, and he'd painstakingly glued himself back together over the last year. It was one of the only things he was personally proud of. He'd fixed himself.

No, it wasn't. He was proud of this farm, that he was able

to care for his dad, and that he'd clawed his way out of the gutter before he'd ruined it all, and he'd done it before Trina had taken a chance on him.

"I know our marriage is done, but I just thought that since we're talking again—"

A hard rapping on the door made them both jump. He spun around and wished he could go back in time and never re-enter the house in the first place. The picture he and Shaylee made looked bad.

He released his ex and turned. Trina glared at him through the door. Brayden inspected Shaylee curiously.

"Hey, Shaylee," Brayden said.

Shaylee returned the smile. Just like her earlier admission, her actions floored him. She'd never had a maternal streak, but the pregnancy must've changed her outlook on kids.

He clicked open the door and shot Trina his most apologetic luck. "Sorry I'm late." He'd been guilty of that too much lately.

Shaylee glanced back and forth between him and Trina, but he didn't see understanding dawn in her eyes. There was no *oh, I interrupted a date*. She looked more like she was anticipating his dismissal of the new arrivals.

"I was just on my way out," he told Shaylee. "We're heading to town for supper."

Shaylee's mouth formed an *O*, but she still didn't look at him and Trina like she thought they were a thing. To her, Trina was probably still the neighbor kid he ran through the fields with.

Did Shaylee think he still carried a torch for her?

"I'll get going." She ran her hands across his shoulders, straightened his collar, then swiped at the wet marks she left on his chest. "You guys have fun. And Lucas, thank you for being there for me."

There it was again. *Thank you for being there for me*. He

gathered on the step with Trina and Brayden, and they watched Shaylee drive off.

"I didn't know she was coming over," he told Trina. "I'm really sorry."

Trina didn't spare him a glance. She tapped Brayden on the shoulders and then went toward the pickup. "Let's go load up."

Lucas joined them and took off to town. The silence in the cab was stifling. Only Brayden chatted about how much he wanted to ride horses and when, and all the hopes and dreams he had for his future with horses. With his grandmas, he could do all of that and more. Lucas kept sneaking glances at Trina.

Out of the corner of his mouth, he asked, "Is everything all right? I know I was a little late."

Trina whipped her head around, the force of her glare hitting him like the broad side of a barn door. If the driver's window shattered from the heat, he wouldn't be surprised. "Of course something's wrong," she hissed under her breath. "But I'm not going to argue about it in front of my son."

Anxiety ate a pit in his stomach. It'd be okay. He'd explain that there was nothing between him and Shaylee. He'd tell her about the funeral and the dentist running off to golf, and she'd understand.

Trina was the only one for him. He wanted to spend the rest of his life with her—he only hoped she'd give him a chance to explain.

HAND HER AN OSCAR, this was the best acting she'd ever done. And it was all for Brayden's benefit.

Hurt continued to lap against her heart like wave after wave onto shore. The sinking pit in her belly when she spotted that too-familiar car had turned to coiled rage at Shaylee curled in Lucas's embrace.

This wasn't jealousy. She didn't think Lucas had romantic feelings for Shaylee anymore.

She was my wife.

Wasn't that the kicker? Just like when they were teens, Shaylee held the lead rope and the other end was knotted around Lucas.

It was one thing to keep her waiting, to make her wonder if she'd been stood up time after time, but it was another to do it to Brayden. On today of all days. Pax had bailed on him for his new woman and Lucas had delayed supper because of his ex-wife.

That was unacceptable.

So she'd played the role of not-quite-fun-loving mother, but at least she was a mom who didn't break plans with her son.

"How was the burger?" Lucas asked Brayden.

"Good. Have you seen the new Transformers movie?" Brayden shoved a fry in his mouth.

Lucas went back and forth with Brayden, like he sensed that she wouldn't talk to him anyway. That was the problem. Lucas was a good guy, and he didn't want to hurt her or Brayden. But she'd not only taken a chance on a relationship, she'd allowed her son to be involved.

No, Lucas being late for lunch or supper wasn't a grievous offense but it was the beginning. Pax had had a beginning too. The moment she'd seen Shaylee's car, she'd been transported to the past. There was always an excuse.

Pax had postponed several dates before he'd started skipping prenatal visits. By the time he'd broken up with her, she'd been practicing her goodbye speech in her head. But Pax hadn't limited his behavior to her. He did the same to Brayden.

A pattern she knew all too well.

There was a reason why she had never opened her life up to a man after him. And sitting here, pretending everything was A-OK, was the main one. The other reasons came after the breakup, and included all the times she was going to have to explain to Brayden why Lucas wasn't coming over anymore or why they weren't going there to see him. She was sure Lucas wouldn't turn Brayden away if the kid ran over to his house to play, but as for the rest, she was going to have to witness the disappointment and answer all the questions.

Taking her time eating her own burger and fries, she mulled over the future conversation she was going to have with Lucas. Dread built inside of her, and she used the feeling to build a wall of resolve. The breakup was going to be hard, but just like when her dad had walked out and when Pax had evaporated from her life, she would move forward and be fine.

"I suppose we should get going," Lucas said after they'd all finished their food. He rubbed his hands on his thighs like he was anticipating the conversation as much as she was. Only for a different outcome.

Brayden made a disappointed sound but Trina nodded. "You have school tomorrow, kiddo."

She had tried to avoid looking at Lucas all night. No matter how she emotionally fortified herself, her resolve wavered when she looked at those brown eyes so full of concern over how things were between them. She eyed those broad shoulders. She fit so well, snuggled into his side. But then she remembered Shaylee cuddled up to him.

She seethed inside. This wasn't about jealousy, but damn. That had burned.

The drive home went too fast, but she formulated all the things she wanted to say. He was about to pull into her place.

She stopped him. "Park in your yard. Brayden can run home."

A muscle in his jaw flexed, but he gave the pickup some gas and idled into his yard and parked in his spot.

Brayden jumped out and petted the dogs, his giggles making her heart break even more.

Brayden broke away from the dogs. "Can I go say hi to Mr. Whiskers?"

"Maybe another time." Trina was going to vibrate out of her skin if she had to wait much longer to get this shit show over with.

Brayden's bony little shoulders slumped, but he charged through the yard and disappeared into her house.

Both she and Lucas stood ten feet apart, waiting for just that moment.

"I didn't know she was coming—"

She stabbed a hand in the air. "I don't want to hear it. Remember when we were kids, how close we were?"

The change in topic made him pause. "You know I do."

"You know what came between us?"

He scratched the center of his chest like it ached. "We got older. I was a guy and got busy with sports and Dad, and you were a girl and…" He lifted a shoulder. "You did your thing."

Just as she'd expected—he didn't understand a damn thing about this entire situation. "No, that wasn't it at all. You started dating Shaylee."

Confusion dimmed his eyes as he frowned. "Are you—"

"Don't you dare say jealous or this conversation is over."

Lucas snapped his mouth shut.

She continued. "Do you remember what I told you about your bachelor party? About how I had to work extra hard to take care of your group, but it wasn't nearly as bad as Shaylee's bachelorette party and how she stiffed me part of the bill?"

From his troubled expression, he didn't recall a damn thing about those parties. "I still don't understand why you never said anything."

"To you? Why would I? We hadn't talked for years. I'm only pointing it out to show you the pattern. You were married to Shaylee and—rightfully so—no other woman existed in your world. That was the way it was since the moment she showed interest in you, only that's the way it *still* is."

He shifted, his boots scraping across the gravel. Jabbing his hands into his pockets, he faced off with her. "I told her that I had to go. I told her—"

"You didn't tell her about me. That's part of the problem. I get that it's none of her business, but when her business is coming between us, then don't you think it's time to tell her that we're dating?" The reservoir of hurt yawned open inside of her. And he was probably confused as hell. "Last weekend, when you were late for dinner because of a phone call, was it her?"

The way his expression shut down gave her the answer she already knew.

"That's the thing. You're divorced. You've been divorced for years." Maybe only two years, but still. "And when she comes around, you're still attached to her lead rope. She says the word, she cries a few tears, and you're still her little Lucas to control. I am not going to put up with that in my life. I'm mad at myself that I was willing to, even when I saw the signs. My celebratory dinner. You driving her home when I was left waiting outside here. You being late because she called. But when it affects my son?" She shook her head. "I have enough to do, trying to heal the damage that boy's father has done and is still doing to him, so I am not willing to tolerate another man who drops his responsibilities as soon as another woman lands on his doorstep."

Lucas was shaking his head. "Her cousin *died*, Trina. I couldn't just kick her out when she's grieving over the death of a kid."

The family death was news, but there were many ways he could've compassionately dealt with Shaylee while respecting boundaries. It wasn't her job to figure it out for him. "You don't get it. She's using you. She's yanking the rope and making you walk or trot to her command. And I think it's even more despicable that she's using a death in the family to do it."

Lucas took a step back and regarded her with wary eyes. "That wasn't what she was doing."

She wanted to growl her frustration into the wind. It'd be as effective. This conversation was…going exactly as she'd thought it would, unfortunately. "You go ahead and defend her, I don't care. I'm done. I'm done with her, I'm done with you, and I'm done with men who don't keep their word."

She spun on her heel and stomped away. Her chest grew tight. This was it. They were over.

As if the dogs sensed the tension, and they probably did, they sat with their tails shuffling against the rocks as they each looked between her and him. She kept walking, and he didn't stop her.

But he did call after her. "Were you just looking for an excuse to end it between us?"

She took one more step before she stopped and looked over her shoulder. His brow was crinkled, his gaze full of disbelief, and his hands were rammed on his hips. But he wasn't coming after her.

"Yeah, that's exactly it. I open myself up to someone after years of being alone and doing everything I could to not grow attached, and I was just waiting, ticking off every time you did something to piss me off, just so I could break things off. That's how I want to end my weekend and go into a week of school and work. Good plan, huh?"

"Trina…"

She left with her name dying on the breeze. Two quiet tears rolled down her cheeks, but she wiped them away before entering her house.

Inside, she put on her brightest smile. "Brayden, let's get ready for bed."

Mom glanced up from the table, her eyes narrowed and lips turned down. "Uh-oh."

"It's over" was all she said.

"Ah, shit, honey. I'm sorry."

Yeah. So was she.

CHAPTER 15

"You look familiar."

Dad had already said that once today. Lucas wanted to close his eyes and sink his head into his hands, but he put a smile on, for Dad's sake.

"I get that a lot." He moved his red checker piece forward a square, remembering the rainy days when he'd sat at his kitchen table as a kid doing the same thing. Same game, same people, but entirely different experience.

It had been a month since Trina had broken up with him. She didn't answer his calls or reply to his messages, and she was a ninja whenever he came to visit Dad. There was never a sign of her, even if her vehicle was parked in the employee section of the parking lot.

The game of checkers wrapped up. Dad couldn't play like he used to. Half the time he forgot the rules and most of the time lately he forgot who his own son was. For Lucas, educating himself on Alzheimer's was one thing, but experiencing it was more devastating than he could've ever predicted.

There'd been too much loss in his life. The paralyzing fear

of knowing he was going to watch his dad disappear before his eyes, followed by the sudden and unexpected death of his mother and the failure of his marriage, and all topped off with Trina.

Shaylee had texted a couple of times in the last month, but Lucas had kept his replies short to keep from encouraging further communication. He was still trying to wrap his head around Trina's accusations.

There was no way that after all this time Shaylee was stringing him along. He'd grudgingly admit that he'd been a puppet to whatever she had desired since the day she'd flirted with him outside of the locker room in high school. But after he'd discovered her betrayal, and the way she'd walked out on him, he'd come a long way. That long road he'd walked all by himself led right over the shadow she'd cast on him.

But Trina was convinced and had left him over it when he hadn't wanted to be insensitive and rude to a grieving, pregnant woman. Ex-wife or not, that just wasn't him, and Trina couldn't accept it. When had she ever known him to be *that* guy?

Putting the checkers away, he considered his options for the rest of the day. There was plenty of work to do at home. Harvest was in, the contract had been filled, he'd been paid, and the desk in his office was piled with plenty of notes and finances to sift through. But he'd been alone in the house for the last month. From the long looks Mr. Whiskers gave him each morning, the big orange tabby felt sorry for him too.

Dad was staring out the window, like he did more and more every day. Lucas sat for a little longer in companionable silence before he said his goodbyes. His heart was heavy as he wove out of the center and he didn't bother trying to catch a glimpse of Trina. If he laid eyes on her, the ball of emotion in his chest might swell and suffocate him.

Aunt Marilyn waited in the doorway of her office as if she'd been on post. "Did you have a good visit?"

He tried to stay strong, to play it off like he could ignore everything he knew would happen to Dad in the near future, but he couldn't. "I wouldn't call it good, but Dad said I looked familiar."

Aunt Marilyn's pleasant expression wavered, offering a quick glimpse into the grief she must experience every day going to work at the same place where her brother deteriorated before her eyes. "He doesn't even say that to me anymore, just asks if I've worked here long."

Look at us. Two adults nearing a breakdown in public.

Lucas stuck his gaze to the floor and went straight out the door to his pickup. Aunt Marilyn's footsteps clicked on the concrete behind him, but she didn't call after him. She was probably as driven to get away from prying eyes as he was.

When he reached the driver's side door, he stopped. "I know I should talk about it, but I really don't want to right now." He *needed* to talk about it, but he was afraid if he opened his mouth, the past fifteen years would vomit out and he'd be left an empty bag of skin. Useless, like always.

"I know," she said. "Same here. But I was hoping to pry into your personal life."

His eyes drifted shut and he tilted his head back. The temperature was near freezing and all he wore was a sweater. Aunt Marilyn had her suit coat on but she didn't look like she was in a hurry to get back to where it was warm. He expected to brush her off, to politely inform her it wasn't her business, but the story spilled out.

He reiterated that awful night in his yard. "Don't you think that's unreasonable of her?"

Aunt Marilyn didn't reply right away. Her gaze swept over the parking lot until it landed on the little sedan Brock and Jesse had found for Trina and fixed up to a point where she wouldn't have to worry about pouring money into it for many more miles. "I think she's one hundred percent right."

Not her too? He was not under Shaylee's spell. "I have no interest in getting back together with her," he said tightly.

"From the sounds of it, neither Trina nor I think you do. But both of us think that when Shaylee calls, you go running."

"She's the one that came out to my place." It sounded weak even to his own ears.

"You've always made excuses for that woman." She shivered and folded her arms across her chest, huddling to preserve body heat.

With a frustrated growl, he opened his door and hit the unlock button, then stuck the key in the ignition. "Hop in and get out of the cold." He fired up the engine and cranked the heat to high.

Once she'd situated herself in the passenger seat, she asked, "Did Trina tell you that I used to be friends with her mom?"

He nodded. The news had stunned him as much as Trina.

"I lost that friendship because I spoke my mind. Before Davina married Nathan, I was honest about what I thought of him and exactly how I thought their marriage would be. And she married him anyway and never talked to me again. So all those years that you were with Shaylee, I kept my mouth shut. You were too precious to me to lose, and I wasn't going to make the same mistake twice. But this time, I guess you and I are both alone, and I would rather risk how you feel about me in order to open your damn eyes and keep you from losing someone who is really good for you—and really good *to* you."

Lucas huffed and tore his attention away from her bold stare. "Tell me how you really feel."

"Oh, I will. Shaylee used you from your first date on, and

she's still using you. Do I think she loved you? Yes. But I think her love is a selfish love, and that she loves herself more. Until she finds someone she's willing to sacrifice for and enter into a give-and-take relationship with, I don't think she'll ever be able to experience true love, but that's none of my business. You are."

"We were too young. We never should've married." It felt weird saying that now. At the time, it had felt so right. Or had it just been because she'd still been there? The idea of living alone on his farm, barely knowing what to do and when because Dad hadn't been around long enough to teach him, was hard to comprehend.

"That was part of it," Marilyn continued. Her voice softer, her approach gentler. "She wanted the country boy with the expensive pickup. You got married and she couldn't adjust to a life that was financially unsteady, or one that didn't provide at the level she expected. And you said she's been in contact with you again? Why not her fiancé?" He opened his mouth to answer, but she held up her hand. "Why not her parents? I'm sure there's an excuse there, and I'm sure you'd make it for her. But the fact is, Shaylee has a life that is separate from yours. So ask yourself *why*. Why would *she* keep coming to *you*?"

"Because we were friends."

"Were you?"

Why would she argue with that answer? But this was Aunt Marilyn, and there was no bluffing her. He thought back on his time with Shaylee. She'd never talked to him until...until after Dad had bought him a new pickup. Lucas had asked her out that day. After that, it was the *getting to know you* phase, then the *falling in love* process, and finally *the family drama* fallout. But married couples were friends, weren't they?

If he needed a sounding board, he went to Aaron. If he

had concerns about farming, he went to Aaron, or Aaron's cousin Justin, or one of the other Walker cousins. His life was farming, and that was what he needed friends for.

With Trina? There was loads of physical chemistry, but he could talk to her. Really *talk*. He lamented about his career. Late at night in the dark when she was curled in his arms, he opened up about his dad. She told him about Pax and how his neglectful treatment of her and especially of Brayden was unforgiveable.

He and Trina were friends, not him and Shaylee.

He pinched the bridge of his nose and blew out a hard breath. "No, we aren't friends."

"You two have a past," Marilyn agreed. "But not a shared friendship. So ask yourself why she's seeking you out."

"She said I was always there for her."

"You are expected to be there when she needs you. The rest of the time, do you really think she cares?"

Accusing Shaylee of not caring about him sounded harsh, but something Aunt Marilyn had said resonated with him. *She loves herself more.* The dentist wasn't raining down the money and affection she thought she deserved, so she was supplementing that void. And he'd fallen for it.

Not only had he fallen for it, but he had a pattern of falling for it. Trina had accused him of abandoning her time and again because of his ex-wife. Looking back, he saw that to be true. Shaylee had never forbidden him from hanging out with Trina, but she had claimed all his free time. She'd consumed him. And when she was done with him, she'd left him and found someone else.

The worst part was how he'd been oblivious to it. Trina had worked his bachelor party and she had worked the bachelorette party, and he didn't even *remember*.

Every phone call, every sudden visit, every interfering

message had devalued Trina. It had discounted her feelings and her importance to him.

He'd fallen hard for Trina, yet he'd trampled over her vulnerabilities.

"I think I fucked up." He dropped his hands across the steering wheel and laid his head on them.

Aunt Marilyn patted his shoulder. "Trina is going to be a tough nut to crack. I saw her coming out of that hard shell of hers, but she's stubborn like her mama. And she's been hurt like her mama."

Unlike her mama, she'd been hurt more than once—her dad and then Pax. And then him.

"She won't even answer a message," he said. "How am I going to apologize? And if I manage to get close enough to her to apologize, how in the world do I get her to take a second chance on me when the only reason she pretended to date me in the first place was because she was afraid you weren't going to hire her?"

She blinked at him. "Pretended to date— Ohhh. And you let me think she was your girlfriend to soften me up?"

He nodded, not guilty at all for what little he'd done for Trina that day. "I kept her up late with my music while I was fixing the Chevy. It was my fault she missed her alarm, but I saw it as my opening with her, and apparently she saw it as her way into the center. Win-win until I messed it up." They sat in silence for a few more moments.

Marilyn spoke first. "Then you're going to have to do something that really shows her you treasure your relationship with her and that the lead rope that she accused Shaylee of tugging has been burned to cinders." She patted him on the shoulder and got out of his pickup.

She made it sound so simple, but it was one of the most impossible tasks he'd faced. In farming, there were grants and programs and experts out there that had helped him get to where he was today. For Alzheimer's, there was a plethora of information on the internet and local professionals to ask. When his mom had died, the community had come together to support him. But fixing things between him and Trina was all up to him. And he wasn't sure he would succeed.

As the principal rattled off instructions for picking up children and wishing everyone a wonderful holiday weekend, Trina scanned the crowd.

Loel was here. His girl was in the same grade as Brayden, but a different classroom. She also spotted Joe and Eva.

The performance officially over, she was making her way to the edge of the temporary bleachers when Loel caught up with her. "Long time no see, buddy."

From the next level down, Mom touched her arm. "I'll go grab Brayden and meet you at the car."

She and Sarah took off for the classroom. Trina stepped to the side with Loel. "Your daughter is quite the performer."

He laughed. "Right? She loves being the center of attention. My ex is grabbing her and then we're going out to dinner."

Trina's smile was bittersweet. Loel and his ex were excellent at the co-parenting gig. His girlfriend was probably working or she would've been here too. Pax was *busy*—his code for "I'm too lazy to go out after five."

Lucas would've come.

Loel saved her from the melancholic wave that usually hit after thinking about Lucas. "We should get the kids together sometime, grill and all that. When the weather's better."

"That'd be fun, but we don't have to wait until spring. Brayden doesn't have many kids around to play with." Not like she'd had.

She was about to wish him a good night and go to the car and meet Mom when two more people joined them.

"Loel." Joe stuck out a hand. "Nice to see you outside of work." He nodded to her. "You as well, Trina, though I don't get to see you as much anymore."

His wife closed their circle. "I heard you went back to school. We miss seeing you, but I'm excited for you. Nursing?"

As she chatted with Eva, Joe and Loel talked Moore sports like they always did when Joe came into the bar. How the varsity football team had done. Whether basketball was going to state this year. Who had gotten volleyball scholarships. Loel had never had an issue making friends with customers. She'd kept them at arm's length.

Why, again?

Because they were all Tonys waiting to happen.

Loel checked his phone. "They're waiting for me. You guys have a good night." He trotted off and she was left with Joe and Eva. Usually, she avoided customers from the bar, having no wish to deal with the awkward chatter after a quick hi. But this was pleasant. How long had Mom been passively pressuring her to get out of her comfort zone of constant work?

Joe turned to her. "Which one was yours, Trina?"

"Brayden was the second on the end. He played a mean triangle. Who were you here for?"

"Our granddaughter is a kindergartener," Eva answered, grandmotherly pride ringing in her voice. "She was the terrified one on the bottom rung."

The rest of the gym was clearing out, but Trina asked about grandkids. Eva was on it with pictures, Joe filled in with stories, and Trina laughed harder than she had in weeks.

Eva glanced around. "I guess we're holding up the

cleaning crew. They all don't have tomorrow off like me and Joe." She started for the exit, still chatting. "Christmas gets so crazy with the grandbabies and traveling to see them all that I've started taking a five-day weekend over Thanksgiving."

Right. Eva was Lucas's insurance agent and Joe was in charge of the county works department. The one with an opening.

Had Lucas applied for the opening? It'd be perfect for him. Part-time, with benefits. Her old manager at the bar, Freddie, had mentioned that Tony was moving away. He felt like he was getting too much shit for his drinking.

While she hoped Tony got help, his departure was good news on two fronts. Bartenders like young and timid Annie wouldn't have to deal with drunk and enraged Tony. And there was now an opening at the county works' shop.

She couldn't help wanting the best for Lucas, or worrying about him.

Stay out of it. Don't do it.

But the crisp autumn air only emboldened her. "Hey, um, I hope Lucas applied for the opening in your department." Smooth, Trina. No one ever said subtle was her strength.

Joe's brows rose in surprise. "Oh, that's right. You two are seeing each other." He shook his head, a shadow crossing his congenial features. "I almost forgot about that night."

"We aren't dating anymore, but he mentioned trying to get a job there before. He'd be good at it." She lifted a shoulder, grateful the lights posted outside the school weren't bright enough to show how badly she was blushing.

Eva tilted her head, her dark eyes more amused than anything. The woman saw right through her.

Joe chuckled and clicked the auto start on his fob. An engine fired at the end of the row. "Well, I'd never ignore a good reference, whether he applied or not." But Joe's grin implied that Lucas had applied and Joe appreciated hearing positive things. Or was that her wishful thinking?

Eva waved toward where Mom patiently waited in the pickup. Mom and Sarah waved back. "It was nice talking to you. At least if we don't see you at Barley 'n' Hops, we can still cross paths at musicals."

"I look forward to it." And, surprisingly, she did.

Walking to Mom's vehicle, she cursed herself for bringing up Lucas. She shouldn't care about what happened with him so much. But not caring about people hadn't saved her from getting hurt. Drifting through life, doing her own thing, was lonely.

Even suffering a breakup, her life was a thousand times better now than it had been this time last year, when she'd only been working and missing her son. She didn't shun relationships like she used to. She still wasn't interested in dating anyone. Just one guy, and someday maybe she'd get over him. Maybe someday, she'd *want* to get over him.

"Yes, sir. Absolutely I'll take the position." Lucas squeezed his other hand into a fist for a silent pump of celebration. He'd gotten the job. Hearing the news on a Sunday night made the long wait over the Thanksgiving weekend worth it.

"Can you start next Monday?" Joe asked.

"Yes, sir." He'd start tomorrow, if needed. It'd delay his plans, but he couldn't pass this position up.

Joe's low chuckle rumbled over the line. "Good, and just call me Joe. We'll get your paperwork done, go over the licenses and certifications you'll need for the equipment you'll be operating. I doubt getting any of them will be a problem since you've been driving farm equipment your whole life."

He'd been driving tractors and grain trucks before he'd had his license—just on the farm, where no one could see. Joe rattled off a list of documents he needed to bring for his first day. When the call was over, Lucas planted his hands on his hips and eyed the stacks of lumber in front of him.

He was on a time crunch now.

The only time Joe would be a hard ass about covering all his shifts would be during the winter when there was snow to clear from school routes. Otherwise, during the summer, Lucas would be grading roads and working on county highways, filling in cracks. Since he was the new guy, he'd probably be shoveling roadkill off the asphalt.

Plywood and two-by-fours, with a few two-by-sixes, were arranged in neat piles in the garage where his Chevy had once been. Lucas scratched his head and looked around the little garage.

It bordered on cold enough inside that he almost needed a heater in here, but if he didn't waste any time, he could get this thing built before the snow fell and the ground froze. He needed to get it in place before the soil was too solid.

Maybe he should've done this project in the shop. No, because then if Mother Nature dumped a foot of snow on the ground, he'd have to move the structure to get his tractor out. And if he finished this thing before the snow fell, then he'd have to figure out how to get the tractor out around it.

Or…he could've driven the tractor out, hauled his supplies into the shop, and once it was done, voila, ready to tow into place. But he hadn't been thinking straight when he'd planned this thing. Getting Trina to take another chance on him was his priority, and this garage had been empty.

At the workbench, he spread out his hand-drawn blueprint. The dimensions might not be accurate. Vaguely, he recalled hanging around Dad when he built little side projects, like the corrals in the barn for the horses. Lucas wasn't constructing the Taj Mahal. Four walls with a door and a roof. He'd just have to YouTube the specifics.

Gus whined outside the door. He cracked it open for the dogs to run in and out. Maybe his next project should be a pet door.

Returning to the workbench, he wrapped a tool belt around his waist and systematically placed his hammer and nails in loops and pouches. The blueprint got stuffed into his front pocket. Once satisfied, he evaluated his project.

Would this even work? If it didn't, then the dogs would have a doggy mansion to claim.

He squatted and arranged the boards for the base. As he was placing his first nail, footsteps crunched outside the door.

Was it Brayden? He hadn't thought up an explanation to tell the kid.

"Knock, knock." Shaylee tentatively stepped inside. She tiptoed until she got in from the worst of the cold, then rubbed her hands together as she surveyed the interior. Instead of the normal distaste he was used to when she was in the garage or the shop, curiosity burned in her gaze.

"What are you working on?" Her belly was even bigger now. The torso portion of her wool coat barely covered the swell of her belly. And instead of the high-quality heeled boots she'd worn during the winters when they were married, she wore sensible nonslip ones. They were probably still high quality, but he wouldn't know the difference.

"I'm…" He wasn't willing to confess what his project was. This Hail Mary to win Trina back was too close to his heart. "Just thought I'd give myself a winter project to stay warm."

She waited like she expected him to explain more—and she probably did. He wasn't going to. As Trina pointed out, he didn't owe Shaylee anything.

He sat back on his heels. "What are you doing here?"

He didn't know if she heard the flatness of his voice. These games of hers were tiring. Her expression went from pleasant to serious. "I came here to talk."

Funny that how after all this time those words still filled him with dread. "About what?" There was nothing for them to talk about. Nothing and no reason.

He rose. The look on his face couldn't be welcoming, and he didn't feel welcoming. Shaylee popping over whenever she pleased didn't sit right. It hadn't before, but thanks to Trina, now he knew why.

"I've been thinking a lot lately." She tucked a strand of hair behind her ear, her gaze darting furtively from ceiling to wall to floor and back. "About you and me."

That was ominous. Ominous, and frankly not his problem. "We're divorced, Shaylee. Have been for a while."

She winced, and her right hand rested on her belly. Looking at her through new eyes, he saw the move for what it was. She wanted his sympathy. She wanted him to fall at her feet, and she knew that her baby was a soft spot. She was trying to manipulate his desire for a family. And she might not be conscious of doing it at all. It was an innate response.

"I made a mistake." Her blue eyes misted over.

He gave himself a moment to reply. His pause was for his benefit, not hers. "I don't think it was."

Her eyes snapped to his. "You don't mean that." When he didn't deny it, her lower lip trembled.

"Were you happy? At all during our marriage, were you happy?"

"Of course I was." She folded her arms over her belly and hugged herself. Just what he thought. She was lying—to him or to herself, it didn't matter.

"I wasn't."

Her mouth dropped open.

He didn't want to hurt her, but he had to be honest. For

both of them. "You were miserable, and it made me miserable. Nothing I did was good enough. No amount of money I made could provide the lifestyle you wanted. None of that has changed."

"That's not true. Not about the money."

"It wasn't just my income," he said quietly. "And then I started seeing someone." Her face fell and she seemed to shrink to half her size, which only made him feel like an ugly ogre stomping on her feelings. "I was almost afraid to…" He took his hat off and shoved a hand through his hair. Saying it out loud took more courage than he anticipated.

"Was afraid to what?"

"Have sex, Shaylee. I was almost too afraid to have sex with Trina because I didn't want to disappoint another woman in bed."

Guilt crossed her face and her gaze darted in the direction of Trina's house. "You weren't bad in bed."

"I know that now. I also know what it's like to be with a supportive partner." He crushed the cap back on his head. "You did a lot of things to hurt me, and I'm only now starting to get over them. I let it affect my relationship with Trina—" He didn't want to share that part of his life with his ex-wife. She already had too much power over what had happened. "That's why I can't have you wandering back in here whenever you feel like it, acting like you want a future with me."

"I was so young when we married," she whispered. "I thought I knew what I wanted, then I didn't. When it was gone, I realized I'd already had it."

"Maybe you just don't have it with your dentist, but be honest. You didn't have the life you wanted with me."

She gazed at him, her lips pressed in a line. "The baby…"

"You'll be a fine mother, but don't use the baby to get your way."

She sucked in a breath, her narrow shoulders squared in defense. "How dare you suggest—"

"I'll dare what I want with my life, Shaylee. I'm sorry, but you're not a part of it anymore. Please leave."

It took more strength than he expected to hold her watery stare. He meant what he'd said, and it was the first time he'd ever talked to her like that. She broke the connection first with a whimper, but she left, her cries floating away in the wind.

It was over. Just like that. He was alone.

But he had a plan and no idea if it'd be enough.

~

"I'm really in a bind. Can you please help out?"

Trina rubbed her temples. Loel wouldn't ask if he weren't desperate. And if it was anybody but him asking, she'd say no. She had three finals to study for and one major test that would decide whether she got an A or B in algebra. "Okay, but this is the last shift until finals are over."

"I owe you big time."

Yeah, he did. Trina pushed away from the kitchen table and gathered her papers and her books. Stacking them neatly to the side where Lucas used to sit, she lined her highlighters next to her pens to avoid the memory of him laughing over Mom's pizza.

Brayden entered the kitchen, beelining for the fridge. "Are you working tonight?"

"Yes. But only because Loel couldn't find anyone to help him."

He poured himself a glass of OJ and leaned against the counter. "Can I go over and play with Gus and Buster?"

Lucas hadn't said anything to Brayden about not being able to play with his animals. She got reports about how Mr.

193

Whiskers was doing, which meant Brayden was also going inside Lucas's house. So many questions welled inside of her, but Brayden didn't mention Lucas asking about her, so she didn't ask about him.

"Tell Gramma or Nana first so they know you're over there." She also had to let them know she was working a few hours tonight.

After a quick chat with Mom, she left for work. It was just a four-hour shift, but she'd been on a roll studying. She'd even been enjoying it. Nearly twelve years had gone by since she'd last had to study, and the novelty hadn't worn off yet. She'd spent too long hoping for the opportunity.

There wasn't much of a crowd at work. She fell into her normal routine: checking on customers, straightening tables, cleaning glasses, and wiping counters. Her job at the center was getting to be the same. She'd greet her coworkers and get to work without having to ask anyone to double-check that what she was doing was right. She could bathe, change, and feed residents in her sleep. She knew the specific needs of each resident, and she'd built a rapport with her coworkers.

She'd miss the bar, but she couldn't wait to start her new career.

She was at the sink scrubbing a shaker clean when she sensed a customer waiting behind her. Not bothering to look behind her, she called, "Be right with you," and finished rinsing the item. She dried her hands with a paper towel and turned around, tossing the wad in the trash.

Oh, shit.

The paper towel bounced off the rim and tumbled across the floor.

Shaylee was across the shiny countertop. Her pert little butt was stationed on a barstool and her hands were clasped in front of her. And she wasn't giving Trina that *I'm ready to order* look.

"What can I get for you?" The politeness came easy. She didn't resent Shaylee. Dislike her for the way she treated Lucas, yes. But the woman was his past, not hers.

Despite how Trina felt toward her, Shaylee's presence amplified the weariness of the last five weeks.

Shaylee glanced to either side of her. The only other person sitting at the counter was on the other side and engrossed in a trivia game. "I went to see Lucas a couple nights ago."

Trina schooled her features into a blank slate. One sentence and she didn't like where this was going.

Shaylee swallowed and her delicate brow crinkled. Was that a flash of regret? "He told me that you two were seeing each other."

This talk was going to happen whether she liked it or not. And she did not like it. "We were." She put her left hand on her hip and leaned on the bar with her right, like she did when she took any other patron's order. Prying eyes wouldn't think they were discussing a highly personal topic.

Shaylee stared at her intertwined fingers. "So you aren't seeing each other anymore?"

The subject of her and Lucas was off-limits to anyone Trina deemed unnecessary. The top of the list was his ex-wife. Lucas could talk to Shaylee about them all he wanted, but she had no obligations, nor did she have any aspirations to share her life with this woman.

"He has some shit to deal with." She shouldn't have offered that much.

Shaylee's sky-blue gaze was direct. "And that shit is me."

That was all she was saying on the subject. She lifted a shoulder. "I have to get back to work—"

"He kicked me out and told me to never come back."

Her hand dropped off the bar. Had she heard correctly? But from the tears welling in Shaylee's eyes, yes, she had.

She didn't know what to say. Too little too late? Would the next time Shaylee showed up at his front door be just like all the others?

"I guess he, uh, doesn't think we were ever right for each other." She took in a shaky breath and visibly gathered herself. She squeezed her eyes shut and rushed out, "Both he and I agree that we married too young, but I guess he's unwilling to forgive the way I treated him and he's moved on already."

Why was Shaylee telling her this? Did she want to hear *I'm sorry*? Not going to happen. Lucas was better off without the emotional manipulation.

Shaylee opened her eyes, pinning Trina once again with her direct gaze. "He's never spoken to me like that. I think—I think he's in love with you."

She clenched her jaw. Her first instinct was to argue. No, he wasn't. *I love you*s hadn't been exchanged before they'd ended things. Trina might've felt it, but her survival instinct had ordered her to keep her mouth shut. For good reason. Having that hanging between them when she'd walked away would've haunted her for years.

The other woman's attention returned to her hands, where her thumbs were rubbing against each other like a one-person thumb war. "He only ever tried to please me, and I threw it all away. Maybe we were wrong for each other, but I don't know that I'll ever be able to find another guy like him. So I hope you're willing to give him one more chance. I won't get in the way."

Feeling like she needed Shaylee's blessing to get back together with Lucas left a sour taste in her mouth. But at the same time, she couldn't believe the woman's admission. Nor could she picture Lucas telling his dainty, pregnant ex-wife to hit the road.

While part of her appreciated the effort of coming in here

and telling her not to fuck it up with Lucas just because she had, it didn't sit well with her to thank Shaylee for giving her the green light.

"I'm sorry, Shaylee, but who I date or don't date and why is my business."

Shaylee's jaw worked, like she was chewing over the words she wanted to say. "I know," she said in a ragged whisper. "But I felt like it was the least I could do for Lucas."

Two more tears tracked down her face as she slipped off her stool and resolutely marched toward the exit.

So. That had been unexpected.

Putting herself on autopilot, she finished out the rest of her shift. Her mind kept wanting to return to what Shaylee had said. *I think he's in love with you.*

She refused to fall for it. She was not going to chase after Lucas just because Shaylee had announced that she was officially done with him. The last five weeks weren't going to be in vain just because Lucas had had one moment of clarity.

But wasn't that the conclusion she'd wanted him to come to? He'd taken the lead rope out of Shaylee's hands and shredded it. He'd not only told Shaylee about her, he'd also told her to quit talking to him. And he'd done it with enough resolve that Shaylee believed it was for good.

Stupid hope. He'd dealt with his unhealthy obedience to his ex. There was no reason for her to read more into it.

Didn't mean she didn't check her phone to see if he'd left a message. No text. No voicemail. No missed calls.

She drove home. The night was clear, yet she was immersed in a fog. With each mile, little gusts of anger grew into a gale-force wind of fury. At Shaylee. At Lucas. At Pax because damn him too.

At herself.

Shaylee had raised her hopes.

She parked outside of her garage and slammed the door.

The noise echoed off the house. She winced and looked up. It was after eleven and only the light in her parents' bedroom was on.

The steady thrum of bass filtered across the yard. The music was barely audible where she stood, as if Lucas knew just the volume to keep from encroaching on the silence inside of her home.

Since that night last summer, he never played his country too loud. She had no reason to go over there. And she was not going to fall at his feet just because he'd given Shaylee the boot. Maybe she was curious about how he was doing. Whether he thought about her. If he was ever going to call her again.

She shivered and yanked her cotton gloves out of her pocket. Something she wouldn't do if she were heading inside.

Damn it.

She stomped across the yard as she put her gloves on. Dried leaves crinkled beneath her boots as she went straight for the detached garage. Was he working on a new vehicle? Hadn't he gotten the job with county works?

She was circling around to the front when she spotted the fall of light across the yard. He had the side door open. Probably for the dogs. But the animals were likely bedded down for the night, having lost interest in Lucas's project.

Since she'd come this far, she stepped inside and stopped. The lights weren't more than a couple of sixty watts, but she blinked several times.

Her shed.

Their shed. The one they had played in when they were kids.

It wasn't the same building. Both of them had witnessed its destruction. This one was new, the wood still a light brown, not gray and weathered. But the size and shape were unmistakable. So was the X built into the back wall, a style Herman Peterson had claimed wasn't about function.

Pounding startled her. Her hand flew to her chest and she looked around. The sound was hammering, but she didn't see Lucas.

She skirted the shed and spotted the opening. No door was attached yet. Scrapes resonated from inside, then more pounding.

She craned her neck to peer through the doorway. Lucas was squatting and nailing a trim board along the floor. His jeans were stretched across his ass, as fine as ever. Despite the chill in the garage, he wore a T-shirt. The blue cloth hugged his shoulders. And she stared for way too long, admiring the flex and bunch of the muscles underneath.

He shuffled to the side and reached into his tool belt. Withdrawing another finishing nail, he positioned it and started swinging, but stopped after two hits.

"Fucking A." A bent nail clattered to the floor and he reached into his pouch for another one.

"Maybe you need to take a break." She bit her lower lip. Had she made the right decision coming over here?

His shoulders stiffened. He eased his hand out of his tool belt and looked over his shoulder. His solemn expression didn't help her acute case of anxiety. Neither of them said anything. He unfolded his strong body.

God, she'd missed him.

"I don't have time for a break. I start my new job Monday."

So he'd gotten the position. The relief flowing through her was for him—and her. He wasn't kicking her out. Yet. "Congratulations."

He shrugged and hooked his hammer in a loop on the belt. Good thing she hadn't seen him like this before, or she might not have had the reserves to stay away from him.

"What are you building this for?" Trina stepped back to get a good look at his unfinished masterpiece and the rigged sleigh he was building it on, presumably to make moving it to its predecessor's position easier.

"For you." He took casual but deliberate steps out of the shed and hopped down when he reached the edge. He landed only feet in front of her.

He was building this for her? An apology? To win her back?

Like he sensed all the questions running through her head, he said, "I couldn't think of another way to show you not only how much you mean to me, but how much you've always meant to me."

The flutter in her belly was so strong, she expected a stupid string of butterflies to leave her mouth when she spoke. "Anything, like tell your ex that you don't want anything to do with her anymore?"

He closed the distance between them. "No, I learned that I had to do that for myself. You were right."

Shaylee showing up at the bar and saying what she had was one thing, the shed was another. But Lucas understanding what their fight was about that night and why she'd broken up with him? Her wildest hopes hadn't matched this outcome.

He tipped her chin up and she leaned into his touch. "I don't know what to do to show you that I'm not like the other men in your life. I can't promise that I won't ever fuck up again, but I can promise that I'll do everything possible to make up for it and to never make the same mistake twice."

He'd said what she couldn't: they were scared. He was terrified of messing up and losing her, and she was afraid to forgive and end up alone anyway.

She peeled her gloves off and stuffed them back into her

coat pockets. Placing a hand on his chest, she asked, "So now what?"

~

DID he dare read into her touch? "I'd like to ask you out on a date, but I know you have finals to study for."

"Have you been keeping track of me?"

"Oh, Tree-bee," he drawled. "I wasn't giving up on us."

He must've said the right thing because she threw her arms around him. He wrapped her in his embrace and buried his face in her hair.

All his senses flooded with everything Trina, everything he'd feared would remain a ghost in his memory. The way she felt against him, her clean, soapy smell, and her short hair tickling his nose.

She tilted her face. His lips touched hers and hovered there for a moment before sinking into her until he didn't know where he stopped and she started.

In sync, he yanked her coat down her arms as she unclipped his tool belt before shrugging out of her jacket. The belt hit the floor with a *thud*. Shirts came off next, landing on top of his tool belt. The cold air in the garage bit into him, but it only drove him to work harder to keep her warm.

He was lost in everything Trina. Warm, soft skin. Her little moans. How well she fit him.

She was yanking on the fly to his jeans. He could be inside her soon. But…where? He consulted the map of his garage in his head. Where wouldn't she get sawdust in undesirable places or grease stains on her ass?

He broke away to stoop down and grab his shirt and his coat. When he straightened, he took in the sight of her.

Flushed cheeks, parted lips, and half naked. Beautiful. Shivers raced across her skin.

He draped her jacket over her shoulders, then lifted his shirt. "Protection."

"Hurry."

"Whatever you want." He backed her up to the workbench, stopping her before she hit the edge. He spread his shirt across the surface behind her.

She skimmed her fingers over his chest, dipping down to each peck. "I've missed you so much."

He touched his forehead to hers as he flicked open the button of her jeans. "My house is so fucking empty without you."

"*I've* been empty without you." She brought his mouth down to hers. He swept his tongue inside and shoved her pants down her legs.

As inch after inch of satiny skin slid under his hands, his erection strained behind his still-closed jeans. She stepped out of her boots and steadied herself against the bench. He finished rolling her pants down her long slender legs. He couldn't help himself. As he squatted down to help her out of her pants, he pressed kisses along the skin of her belly, down her shapely thighs, until finally she was bared before him.

She whipped off her bra and tossed it on the workbench.

Desire darkened her eyes. "Are you gonna make me wait much longer?"

"No, ma'am." He needed to keep them both warm.

He kissed his way back up. Crowding close to her, he ripped open his jeans and shoved them down only far enough to let his cock spring free. She anchored her hands on the edge of the workbench as he lifted her and settled her butt on the edge.

He hooked his arms under her spread legs and wrapped

them around his waist. Without hesitation, she gripped his length and guided it to her entrance.

This wasn't just a quick fuck. This was a reconnection, and he wanted her to feel it as much as he did. Slicking himself in her heat, he made sure she was ready.

Looking her straight in the eye, he pushed inside with one smooth thrust. She clenched around him, her hands digging into his shoulders as she rocked against him. That was all he needed. He pounded into her as much as he could. Her legs were hooked around him so tightly he could barely thrust, but this wasn't about getting off.

Five weeks apart. She didn't need him and he didn't need her, but they wanted to be together until they couldn't be apart.

The way she gripped him, her muscles rippling around his shaft, was more than he could take. "You drive me crazy."

"Is that your way of saying that you're not going to last long?" she panted. "Because I'm not either."

He let out a growl. Stroking into her as much as their position would allow, he kept his climax at bay until she cried out his name. Heat flooded over his cock until he thought he would combust. The crest of his orgasm crashed into him. He gave one last thrust, spilling his release inside of her. Everything drained out of him. The stress of losing her. The frustration of not knowing what to do. The fear that he wasn't good enough and never would be.

But he was filled at the same time. The pit of emptiness inside of him when she walked away. The loneliness of lying in bed without her. The need to talk to her each night, not about the important stuff. About her work. His job. The interview. She overflowed those spaces inside of him.

He buried his head in the crook of her neck and wrapped his arms tightly around her as he finished coming. She clung to him, her arms holding him as tight as her legs. At some point, the jacket had fallen off, but they made their own cocoon of heat.

They stayed in the same position as they came down from their climax. He was still hard, but the next time they were together he wanted her spread across his bed.

Or his couch.

Anywhere but in the garage.

He stayed inside of her as he met her gaze and uttered words he'd never thought he'd get to say to her. "I love you."

This might not have been the best time for a declaration, his ass hanging out in the wind while he had just taken her on the workbench of his garage, but he wasn't willing to wait any longer to let her know how he felt.

Her legs twitched, rocking her against his length. "I love you too."

The biggest grin spread across his face. "So the shed worked then?"

Her head went back as she laughed. He couldn't leave her graceful neck alone.

Maybe they wouldn't make it to the house before the next time after all.

EPILOGUE

*D*riving home after class, Trina studied the nice clean lines of snow built up on each side of the road, a wide swath of clear gravel bordered by straight walls of the dirty snow that had been pushed away. Was Lucas the one who'd plowed today?

During the last few months, her routine hadn't changed, but so much else had. She went to school, worked at the center, and picked up the occasional bar shift. Lucas worked three days a week and odd hours during a storm, but otherwise he either came to her place for supper or she and Brayden were invited to his.

Brayden didn't ask to go to Lucas's anymore. He only had to let someone know where he was going, even if it was safe to assume that he would be where the dogs were.

She'd started her new semester of classes, and Lucas gave her plenty of room to study. He was her biggest supporter and she hadn't thought that was possible. Mom and Sarah were excellent cheerleaders, and Brayden might be blasé about her career change, but he was thrilled at the change in their life. Animals, outdoors, and getting spoiled by grand-mas. Not much more a kid could ask for.

Except a horse. She wouldn't be surprised if Lucas used his connections to get a good deal on a nice pony for her son this summer. Lucas's attentiveness took the sting out of Pax's lack of interest, and Brayden didn't beg his dad to spend time together as often. Bittersweet, but that was the way it was.

She pulled into her yard. A smile tugged on the corners of her mouth. Every inch of the driveway was scraped of snow. Sarah might be fearless using the bucket to clear the drive-way, but that didn't stop Lucas from doing a sweep through when he cleared his property.

She trotted up the porch steps, and once her foot hit the top, the front door swung open. Mom, Sarah, and Brayden piled onto the porch.

"What's going on?" Trina didn't want to linger outside. It was a normal February day in Minnesota, which meant it was well below zero with a wind that chiseled the top layers of skin off her face.

"Nothing," Mom said. "But we're going out to eat."

Something was up. Mom checked her watch. Sarah met her questioning look with a steady gaze. Trina eyed Brayden. He had the weakest poker face and right now it screamed *I know something you don't know.*

"You guys aren't talking."

Sarah's grin was unrepentant. "Get in the pickup."

Trina did, not bothering to ask questions on the way to town. Brayden was so excited he was jittering out of his seat. She didn't want to ruin it for him. Mom and Sarah might be able to keep the secret, but he would fold like a wet towel.

They pulled up to Tyler's and parked in the lot. But when they towed her inside, they didn't stop at a booth or a table. The door to the party room in the back was open and the lights were on.

The other three fell back as she entered. Curly streamers hung from the ceiling, and a royal-blue tablecloth was topped with a sparkly silver sign that read *Congratulations!*

From behind her, Brayden yelled, "Surprise!"

"There she is," Joe boomed. His wife gave her a little wave from where they were seated with Loel.

Janie was at the table next to them, chatting with Marilyn. Lucas's aunt had been to her house once since the new year. Trina had told her Mom about Marilyn's break-room confession and they'd started talking again.

Janie came to greet her. "My parents took me out to dinner last night after I gave them the good news. Now I'll have to ask them why I didn't get the royal treatment."

Trina let out a nervous giggle. This was all for her. These people were here for her? "I only got into nursing school. I didn't graduate."

Lucas was at the end of the table with his arms spread out. His grin was as lopsided as it could get. "And wait until you see *that* party."

He had organized a celebratory dinner in her honor. The last time he'd missed out, but not now. This time he'd *planned* it.

By the time she'd made her rounds greeting everyone, the food had been rolled in, buffet-style. Chicken wings, cottage fries, coleslaw, and a sheet cake that wasn't just a generic purchase from the grocery store. Her name and the start date of nursing school were in cursive script across the top.

She filled her plate and took a seat by Lucas.

He slid a card toward her. "I caught Dad on a good day. He signed the card."

The card nearly toppled the dam holding back her swell of emotions. Herman's shaky signature wasn't legible, but it was there.

"I told him that you and I were together and that maybe

someday you'd even convince me to marry you." He winked and stuffed a fork into his coleslaw.

She elbowed him. "I'll keep working on it."

He'd already asked her. Not in a sweeping gesture like this party, but in an honest conversation to find out what she wanted. What he did was exactly what she'd wanted—no pressure until school was done, which was a little over a year away. Then maybe she'd do distance learning to get her RN degree.

She'd told him some time in there would be good to expand their family if he still wanted kids.

Don't have more kids just for me. What do you want? he'd asked.

I never had a reason to think about having more kids. Now I do, and maybe in a year, you know, we can try.

No matter what happens, it won't change how much I love Brayden.

Damn, she almost teared up thinking about how solemn he'd been.

Lucas interrupted her train of thought. "Have you been to the shed lately?"

"There's, like, a foot and a half of snow."

He tipped his head toward Brayden. "Not in the path he's tamped down with the dogs. They have quite the fort going on in there. Transformers, Matchbox ramps, and Legos."

So that's where the toys had been disappearing to. "Too bad there's no neighbor kid for him to play with."

Loel sauntered up to them. "I've been hearing a lot about this fantastic shed from your boy. I wish I had a fort like that for the munchkins. They get bored when they're over to visit. Nothing but ol' dad to entertain them."

"Why don't you bring them over sometime?" she asked.

Lucas ducked his head. "Trina mentioned your girl's the

same age. We've got dogs, a fat cat, and the fort. Your son would have a good time too. We can grill and let them roam."

Loel looked like he thought it was too good to be true. "You're sure it's no problem? I don't want to intrude."

She could picture Brayden's whoop of excitement now. "Our closest neighbors are almost a mile away. It'd be good for Brayden to have a kid or two his age to play with out there."

Lucas nodded and shot her a knowing look. "Best thing that's ever happened to me."

She smiled and clasped his hand. "Me too."

————————

DID you catch the book that started it all? The first of five cousins that farm and ranch together has to work harder than ever to win the woman of his dreams. Conflict of Interest is available at all retailers.

IT'S ALWAYS the right time of year for a holiday novella. Moore's favorite veterinarian might lose her business in Her Christmas Offer.

I'D LOVE to hear what you thought. You can drop a quick review for Rancher Next Door off at the retailer.

FOR ALL THE LATEST NEWS, sneak peeks, quarterly short stories, and free material sign up for my newsletter.

ABOUT THE AUTHOR

Marie Johnston writes paranormal and contemporary romance and has collected several awards in both genres. Before she was a writer, she was a microbiologist. Depending on the situation, she can be oddly unconcerned about germs or weirdly phobic. She's also a licensed medical technician and has worked as a public health microbiologist and as a lab tech in hospital and clinic labs. Marie's been a volunteer EMT, a college instructor, a security guard, a phlebotomist, a hotel clerk, and a coffee pourer in a bingo hall. All fodder for a writer!! She's married with four kids.

mariejohnstonwriter.com
Facebook
Twitter @mjohnstonwriter
Instagram @mariejohnstonwriter

www.ingramcontent.com/pod-product-compliance
Lightning Source LLC
Chambersburg PA
CBHW050359190726
48284CB00007BB/2351